THE
COURTING
OF
KINGDOMS

ISBN-13:

- Standard Hardcover: 978-1-959427-29-2
- Standard Paperback: 978-1-959427-27-8
- Foreshadow Special Edition: 978-1-959427-38-4
- Ebook: 978-1-959427-28-5

Cover Design by Fantasy Cover Design

Edited by Unbound Literary Editing

Interior Formatting by Rebecca K. Sampson

THE COURTING OF KINGDOMS

R.K. SAMPSON

For those who wonder:
Would it be fun to date a prince? How about two?

The Courting of Kingdoms is a *Lightlark* meets *The Selection* romantasy love triangle where thirty women compete to break the curse, marry the prince, and save their kingdom.

Madeline was content to live a quiet life, filling her days working, reading, and playing with her neighbor's child. She wasn't happy, but she was safe. And in a kingdom like Riversend, trapped by the Ageless Blight, safety was enough.

Within the palace walls, however, nothing is as it seems. A prophecy claims a commoner will marry the second-born prince and break the curse, and Madeline is chosen as one of thirty women to compete for his hand. But as she draws closer to the prince, Madeline's heart wavers toward his brother—charming, forbidden, and full of secrets.

Two princes. One deadly choice. Will love save their kingdom or doom it forever?

CONTENT GUIDE

Content in The Unending Kingdoms may be triggering
for some readers. Reader discretion is advised. Learn
more on rksampson.com/content-guide

THE PROPHECY

AS TOLD IN THE SCROLLS OF THE QUEEN:

No life sprouts forth,
nor death takes hold—
Unending youth mirrors
the reign we've foretold.

'Twas a dreadful curse,
an Ageless Blight,
as the wheel halts
a millennium for respite.

While some may heal,
the rest will fester
with allies in their tomb.
The unfolding trickles blood
in the tapestry of wounds.

Befalling the trials
of love's stead
The Summer Maiden
learns the truth of the dead
with the second-born prince
enthralled and newly wed.

Together they hold
two souls, two paths—
a curse lifted or restored.
Woven in dread
her heart
must be forged.

Entwined in stolen grief
their crowned paths may be,
for all and for each other,
for one loves the other
in a tale
of sight and gold.

When the dead rival the living,
it all comes to be
for it's now or never
to bring upon the prophecy.

CHAPTER ONE

Arabella turned her gaze from the snow-covered hills outside their window, her hands trembling as she gripped the edge of the table. "When pain goes on forever, what makes life worth living?" she asked, her voice cracking. Tears streamed down her cheek, and she sniffed. It wasn't fair, none of it was. The moment happiness kissed their cheeks, it was taken away, leaving behind only blood and tears.

"You do," Ambrose said, as if it were the only answer. "Decades of pain is a small price to pay for even a moment with you." He reached for his love, wrapping his arms around her.

"I wanted more time," she whispered, the sun setting behind her.

Ambrose smiled lightly, tucking her hair behind her ears. "We'll have more time, in this life or the next."

It was a promise she knew was empty, but she let the hope of it linger in her heart, as they waited for the knock on the door that they knew was coming.

A lone tear trailed down my face, and I angrily wiped it away. I don't know why I let these books get to me. Love wasn't worth forever, not in the Kingdom of Riversend.

But Apes Matthews wanted me to believe it was true. He published three romance novels each year the Ageless Blight has trapped us. Each claimed love would prevail, but that was fiction. Just like the goddess of love, Miran, people were fickle.

In reality, he was just a good storyteller. Love wasn't going to save us.

I couldn't bear the thought of falling in love, only for that person to leave me after a century for someone else, like was the story of many couples since the blight. It seemed long-term commitment was only possible when life was finite.

But dissociation from reality was my favorite activity, so I read every book I could get my hands on, finding an escape in what could never be. Reading about love was better than experiencing it myself. Every fleeting relationship I had over the years met the same fate. After a while, it was easier to not try.

Closing the book, I put it away in my bag. My lunch break from the bakery was almost done. It was the latest in a string of jobs I didn't care about, but at least I didn't need to do any of the baking. I just sold the sweet treats and got to take a few home at the end of the day. I can't remember the last time a job fulfilled me. I needed to eat after all, and getting free treats and money while selling pastries for a high markup wasn't a bad way to pass the time.

Wiping invisible dust off my dress, I walked down the cobblestone streets of Everbrook and away from the shady tree I liked to sit under. I've spent all of my life in this small village, and I liked it that way. Familiarity gave me the comfort of knowing the variables. I could make choices each day, knowing what to expect.

Every house appeared both new and old. With one thousand years of living, no additional people in the workforce, and the Deadlands growing at an alarming rate—the entire kingdom was a patchwork. We tried to be innovative in the beginning, but there was little incentive in a world that stayed still, forsaken by the god of age, Thailor. With the promise of tomorrow, there was no reason to change today.

Sort of promised, anyway. The dead continued, dubbed the Unending, but they weren't the same.

Now, our world was devoid of joy. And the laughter... I never heard it anymore. There were no children untouched by this curse. Even with their limited understanding of what has happened, it's like every bit of happiness was sucked from the room a child walked into.

Nothing was wonderful anymore.

When the Ageless Blight first started, we were unsure how long it would last. It was initially seen as a miracle, and there was joy in seeing those we loved spared from death. But as time continued, everyone came to realize the true cost. At first, people kept their deceased at home, to try and soak in whatever extra time they were given. But after a while, there was no space for the Unending. And those that perpetually bled? They were difficult to care for.

That was why the Crown created the Deadlands, a new city (now, multiple cities), to keep the dead in one place. We're told it's more humane for them there, a calm place for the Unending to rest.

No one wanted to talk about it, how the Unending

were close to outnumbering the living. Compartmentalizing was common.

Especially since they began mirroring. It was whispered, if you saw someone with yellow eyes, you had to run.

I didn't like thinking about it.

The bakery was in sight a few minutes later, but the street looked wrong. A crowd had gathered in the middle, surrounding a sleek black carriage. Why were so many people here?

"News from the great Queen Arika Komari! Announcement from the queen! Gather here!" a man said, standing on the driver's seat, waving a scroll in the air. I couldn't see much of him from my vantage point.

We didn't hear from the royal family as often as we used to, nor has there been someone here to tell us the news in person in years. In the beginning of the Ageless Blight, there were new rules we had to learn every week. It took a while to set up our society around our new limitations. The last dozen rules all had to do with governing the Unending. The regulations were usually received in a list, mailed to our houses rather than shared by a representative.

When your death could mean being in pain forever, the most paranoid (and the most important) kept away. With the kingdom at stake, and no further heirs possible while we stayed trapped in time, the royal family rarely left the grounds.

The village folk must have also felt the unease. They shuffled out of the storefronts and from up and down the street until we were a larger crowd before him. Not wanting to be trapped between so many bodies, I found a bench and sat down off to the side. It was close enough that I should hear everything. Murmurs grew as we waited for him to speak.

"Citizens of Riversend, we have information to share about the Ageless Blight," the representative said, his head above the rest. "The Crown's prophets have a new prophecy that speaks of our ailments, as well as a way to break what binds them. We will send a copy to every doorstep to read."

A hush fell over the crowd as people leaned forward, eager to hear more about this prophecy that could change everything. Why is it showing up now, a thousand years later? With each word, my heart beat faster.

"Important details in this prophecy point to a woman within our realm that can break the curse, and please the god of age, along with the help of our beloved Prince Reignold Komari. Together, they will end our suffering," the representative continued.

Our first queen and king were chosen based on such

prophecies, their family line divinely chosen. Many people in the kingdom had boasted they could see and tell fortunes, and it's common knowledge that witches and prophets still advised the royal family and other political leaders, but a prophecy for how this could all end? No one had made that claim before. It was a dangerous one to make, after all. If you were wrong, you signed your own death warrant. Permanent death, that is, reserved for treason and the most dangerous of criminals. *Decapitation.*

Angering the royal family was ill-advised.

The representative held up a hand to request silence before he continued, "To help these events come to fruition, we are inviting thirty women to the castle to stay and compete for Prince Reignold's hand in marriage. The winner of the competition will become our princess, join the royal family, and save us all. Our queen urges us to understand that while it may not be obvious why each of these women were chosen, trust that our wisest advisors, prophets, and energy readers have reviewed all angles to decide who is most likely to meet the prophecy's needs."

The murmurs grew louder and people started shouting questions at the representative. A competition? This seemed like an odd way to choose a wife, but it must be part of the prophecy somehow.

"We are almost through with what has plagued us. The time for healing and planning our next chapter is soon to begin." The man took a deep breath before rolling the paper up and surveying the crowd.

"Before I hand out the prophecy," he said, holding the scroll in the air like a flag, "there is one citizen of Everbrook that meets the criteria and must leave with me to the palace."

My eyes widened, fingers clenched in front of me. *Who was it?* I looked at the women in the crowd, some were pushing through to get to the front, excited at the prospect of marrying the prince. Others gripped the hands of those around them, seemingly nervous and not wanting to be chosen. Getting picked to potentially wed the prince when you're already married would be quite an embarrassing situation. Would they dissolve any marriage they needed to get women for the prince?

He pulled a folded paper from his satchel and I held my breath, looking into the crowd instead of at him. Who was going to save us?

"Is Madeline Parch in the crowd today?"

As every face turned to find mine, the blood seemed to drain from my body. I stood on wobbly legs, stiff with shock. Walking toward him, I stuttered, "Wh-what? Me?" My eyes blinked rapidly at the stranger, shocked to be addressed.

"If you are Ms. Parch, then yes. You have one day to pack up and then you are leaving with me. Meet me at the inn tomorrow at dawn," he said and jumped off the carriage, passing out the flyers that sat upon it. Few people looked at it, their eyes fixed on me instead. Some were envious, others pitying.

When he handed one to me, along with a letter about my required participation, the words blurred together.

"Why her?" a townsman asked, loud enough for all to hear.

Even though they weren't talking to me, I answered.

"I don't know."

CHAPTER TWO

Numb, I opened the door to my small home, skipping the rest of the shift at the bakery without notice. How I made the walk back, I don't know. My head was buzzing, unable to comprehend the card fate had dealt me.

It was not difficult, however, to imagine what the town was gossiping about now.

The small, broken town of Everbrook has a champion, but it was that weird, quiet girl who has no friends and hasn't had a lover in decades. I wonder, why her? Shouldn't someone more interesting be the subject of prophecy?

They weren't wrong.

Looking at the note the representative gave me, I read it again.

Madeline Parch,

You have been summoned to participate in the removal of the Ageless Blight, as dictated by the royal advisors in their divine prophecy.

Attendance is required upon penalty of permanent death. The victor of the prince's heart will be named Princess of Riversend, betrothed to Prince Reignold Komari, second in line to the throne. All participants, regardless of whether or not they win, will be henceforth known as Curse Breakers.

It went on for a few paragraphs of flowery language, presenting why this was such an honor for me. Other than the first two lines that told the truth of the message, the panic and desperation of our need to end this curse once and for all, the rest was a public relations move.

We're ready to move on. The prophecy reveals that now is the time, and one of our people will join us as fate-chosen to rule.

Prophecies, star-destined, fate-chosen, whatever the royal family wanted to call it, hadn't stopped the world from going into chaos a thousand years ago. The royal family, ordained generations ago by destiny—*their* prophets—to rule Riversend, claimed that no prophet had information about the Ageless Blight before. And now they did. How convenient.

> *Our future princess is the only one who can break the curse.*

They dangled the carrot.

> *If those chosen to compete do not comply, they will be charged with treason.*

The stick threatened.

There was so much unanswered. What was I expected to do in this contest? What if who was meant to break the curse was actually not who won the competition? What if they sent the true Curse Breaker home?

I picked up the letter again and stared, looking for any other way out of this, but of course there was none. Putting it aside, I opened the scroll that detailed the prophecy. I couldn't contain my curiosity any longer. What would it say about me?

In a curling script, it read...

No life sprouts forth,
nor death takes hold—
Unending youth Mirrors
the reign we've foretold.

'Twas a dreadful curse,
an Ageless Blight,
as the wheel halts
a millennium for respite.

While some may heal,
the rest will fester
with allies in their tomb.
The unfolding trickles blood
in the tapestry of wounds.

Befalling the trials
of love's stead
The Summer Maiden
learns the truth of the dead
with the second-born prince
enthralled and newly wed.

Together they hold
two souls, two paths—
a curse lifted or restored.

Woven in dread
her heart
must be forged.

Entwined in stolen grief
their crowned paths may be,
for all and for each other,
for one loves the other
in a tale
of sight and gold.

When the dead rival the living,
it all comes to be
for it's now or never
to bring upon the prophecy.

I read it three times, looking for clues, and found barely anything workable. How could the supposed Curse Breaking Committee think this was about me? Or at least, someone like me. There was barely anything that described the Summer Maiden. I was born in the summer, but surely many women were.

Dread was alive in me, taking over my body. I didn't want to marry the prince and be a public figure for the rest of my life. This couldn't actually be about me anyway, so if I left, someone else could work on the curse. Could I run away? They would decapitate me if I ran, but that could only happen if they found me. I'm a nobody, I could hide in another town far away...

What would be worse, permanent death if I'm caught or joining the royal family if the prince took a liking to me? For the reclusive person I was, both felt equal in measure. I may want to die, technically, since I want the curse lifted and age restored, but that was different. If I became the princess, my life would be under their control. How I sat, what I said, how I dressed, what I did... My children would be subject to the same fate. It was a cage, a golden one, but a cage nonetheless.

Having my head cut off was not the same thing as growing old, but that would be a quicker death than being a princess.

Surveying my living room, I took in the life I had built over a thousand years. A couch I have to update every ten years. A thirty-year-old bed and mattress that felt lumpy. Books on every surface. Paintings of rivers and forests that helped add to my calm. Blankets, *all over*. And a chest in front of my bed that held things that belonged to my parents. I hadn't opened it in hundreds of years because of the fragility of our old life. Much of what was in there would crumble at my touch. Everything of importance that I kept from my parents was in there.

The weight of these stagnant years was difficult to handle. Items wore out, and you replaced them. People grew weary, but they mostly lived on. Bitterness festered, but there was an eternity to fix things. Life continued on, yet it never truly did. Moms couldn't see their kids grow up. Adults saw their parents get hurt and die, yet continue to suffer. And the youth? It was torture to never have the chance to become more.

I'm grateful I was in my twenties when the curse hit, free from the eternal education that the perpetual children and youth had to endure because the curse happened before their brains fully developed. It wasn't fair for them. For anyone.

Resigned, I realized *I had to go.* If I hid, I would always wonder. Not about the prince, of course, but if I could have helped the perpetual children. If the Crown's plan failed and the curse became everlasting, I'd never forgive myself.

There was no use crying over what I could not change. Okay, I cried a little, but mostly on the walk over. I needed to bow to fate now. Sifting through my closet, I took out a travel bag and filled it with the highest quality clothing I had. It wasn't much, unfortunately, but it would have to do. What does one wear to date a prince? Nothing I owned, that's for sure.

Next, I looked through my books. Hopefully, I would survive this, and could come back to my books, but for now I decided on two books to bring. One was my favorite romance from Apes Matthews, with a worn out spine, that I could binge in case of emergency. It was one of those depressing ones, more dark than would be appropriate in real life, but still my favorite.

The second, a book on the royal family and their traditions. It was an older edition, but it could guide me on when was the right time to bow versus curtsy and random facts like the prince's middle names. It also had a chapter dedicated to the life of the king before he passed. That may come in handy. Maybe there would be some sort of prince quiz in this mysterious contest. They eventually recalled and reprinted this edition to have updated information throughout the Ageless Blight, but I'm sure the base information was still factual.

These wouldn't be enough to entertain me when I had time alone, but hopefully the castle would grant me access to their library. I bet they have hundreds of books I've never even heard of.

The library and the likely very comfortable beds might be reason enough to enter this competition willingly. I could go, see who was nice from the contestants, and help them win while I enjoyed reading and sleeping as much as possible. It's not like the prince would pick me out of twenty-nine other women. I didn't want a relationship, with him or anyone, so he'd move on fast.

Were books really the only reason I wanted to stay alive?

Having a general plan, even a silly one, helped me feel better about the situation.

A few hours of pondering later, my books chosen, my toiletries packed, shoes selected, house locked up, and I was ready to go. There was no way I could wait calmly until tomorrow. Hopefully the royal representative wouldn't mind leaving early.

Before I left to go to the inn, I made one more stop. Turning down the sidewalk, I walked toward my neighbor's porch. I knew she'd already be sitting there, like she always did at this time of day. Hester Sutherland loved to have her lunch outside with a cup of tea, her granddaughter playing beside her.

Her mother was in the Deadlands.

"Hello, dear, where are you off to?" she asked, eyeing my bag with a squint. She was right to be suspicious, she and I rarely went anywhere. We were the quiet ones of Everbrook, staying in our corner, leaving everyone alone.

When it came to lack of progress, I knew I was part of the problem in our society.

Flora sat on the floor beside her, playing the same block game I saw her with every day. Flora was two, but she didn't act like it. After the first few years of the Ageless Blight, she stopped speaking. Instead, day in and day out, she hit her blocks. In different shapes, the child was supposed to fit them into the right holes, like a puzzle. She couldn't figure it out, and instead hit the block on top of each hole, not remembering or being able to work out where it was supposed to go, despite doing it daily for decades.

We watched her hit the triangle block on the circle hole, again and again, until she moved on.

"I've been summoned to the castle as a potential Curse Breaker," I said, waving my paper around.

"What?" she asked, voice slow and crackling. Her dark weathered face pinched, as if that would change what she heard.

Figuring she didn't know the gossip, I started to explain. "The palace chose thirty women—"

"No," she interrupted and shook her head. "I know what it's for. They passed out notices at the store. But why you? You're nobody."

The words stung, though they shouldn't have. She was right, and I knew it.

"I know." I shrugged. "Apparently, a group of advisors or prophets or who knows what, think I suit the profile."

"I'm sorry, dear. I wish you wouldn't go."

"Why sorry?" I asked. Most people would see this as a good thing, even if a few were jealous or confused about why I was chosen.

"I'll never see you again," Hester said with a sad tilt of her head.

"No, I'll be back in a few weeks," I said with a small smile. "Don't worry."

"You aren't coming back," she said. "One way or another. I'm sorry. And this old bag of bones?" She scoffed, gesturing to herself. "Even if you did, I'll probably drop dead the second the curse is lifted."

I swallowed thickly. "Don't say that. You'll be fine, so will Flora, and I'm coming back. Now, Hester, can you give me a hug goodbye? I was hoping for comfort, not more dread."

"Sorry, dear, you should have known you wouldn't get anything but the truth from me," Hester said, though she did come forward to pull me into her arms.

"I know. I love you for it," I said, smiling into her hair as I held tight.

"Now stop feeling sorry for yourself and go," the elderly woman said and pushed me back. "Get a crown so you can help those idiots in the royal family know what the little people want."

"It's not like I'd get to be queen, Hester. The winner gets the spare, not the heir." It was a cruel phrase, but it was accurate.

"That's a better deal, if you ask me," she said with a click of her tongue.

"Maybe, but I don't intend on winning. I'll help whoever is there and then leave," I explained. "Things will be better afterward, for all of us."

Bending down to kiss the top of Flora's head, I pointed where the triangle block should go. Maybe she'll understand it by the time I get back.

"We'll see, we'll see. Don't dawdle." Hester gestured to the street. "I don't want to see your face here anymore."

I listened and backed up, walking down the steps, closing the gate to her property and making my way down to the main road. I glanced back and she was still there on the porch, gripping her tea in wrinkled hands, watching me go. With a parting wave, I turned around and willed myself not to look back again.

CHAPTER THREE

There were people gathered all along the street in clusters, discussing the prophecy and *me*. Their voices buzzed like restless bees, looking for pollen for their missing queen. Meanwhile, my heart pounded against my ribcage.

"What do you think this part means?" one person asked. "Obviously it must be..." muttered others, though they didn't seem as assured as the statement implied. A common one was, "Why her?" and the most hilarious, "Could she have used witchcraft to get picked?"

I was basically the town hermit. Why would they think I wanted this? Walking quickly past the crowds, I turned into the alley and kept to the shadows. It took longer to get the inn that way, but it would be quieter.

The dust from the walk gathered along the hem of

my lilac dress. I stared at it nervously, wondering what the palace would think of me arriving in dirty clothes.

Everbrook's only inn was a modest two-story structure with a thatched roof and weathered wooden exterior. It was cozy and well-kept, with a bar for entertainment next door. Having known the innkeeper all my life, I knew she took pride in being the only place visitors could stay. And now, she had the honor of hosting the representative of the queen. Even though we weren't friends, I was happy for her.

Not a lot of people understood that. You could want the best for people and still want nothing to do with them. You could even hate them and still wish them well.

I let her know I was here and waited in the lobby for her to deliver the message to his room. A few people lingered, their eyes shifting to me, but thankfully I didn't have to wait long. It was uncomfortable being so exposed.

"You packed up quickly," a voice said.

I turned, finding the thin man who had told me the life-changing news only hours before. He was shorter than me by a foot, rail thin, with dark olive skin and cropped brown hair. His face was kind, and I couldn't tell when I watched his announcement, but up close I saw his eyes were hazel.

"What's your name?" I asked, smiling. Hopefully, we could be friends, or at least friendly. I'd know no one else in the castle.

"Mitchell," he said, extending his hand to shake. Mitchell had a firm grip and a quiet authority to him, something that was impossible to replicate. He just was, and part of me hoped one day I'd feel that too.

"Hi, Mitchell, thank you for being my escort. If it's alright with you, I'd rather leave now than wait for morning," I said with a half smile and shrug. "If you don't, it's okay, I'll just get a room. I don't want to go back home and stare at the wall."

"Of course, I would love to get there sooner too. Is that all you are bringing?" he asked, nodding at the small bag on my shoulder.

My skin flushed. "Yes, I don't have many items appropriate for the palace."

"That's alright," he said with a nod. "They've been shipping in dresses and other supplies for *weeks*. We'll have everything you need." His voice inflected as he said weeks, as if he found it funny. I imagined the grand halls of the palace, filled with mountains of silk and lace, all waiting to be worn by strangers like me. If they planned to clothe all thirty women, that would be hundreds of dresses, if not over a thousand. It depended on how long they thought we'd all stay.

"How did they know what sizes to bring?" I asked, following him as he settled his tab at the front. The innkeeper waved him off, saying there would be no charge, and we went on our way.

"They've known all year who the women would be," Mitchell explained. "They wanted to make sure everything was in place as early as possible, but preparation is important to the royal family, so there were other projects to get the palace ready first. With this being the kingdom's only shot, they didn't want to take any chances. As for the clothes, that was the last step. Knowing that not every potential princess came from wealth, they wanted to even the playing field. We don't want any first impressions to be impacted by something as easily fixed as an outfit."

I'm clearly not very observant if I didn't notice people spying on me, guessing my size, so they could prep the dollhouse I'd live in. It was equally as disturbing as it was curious. Was the prince vain enough that how each Curse Breaker looked would matter to him? Hopefully, it wouldn't become common knowledge that they've had the prophecy for a year. I'm sure the kingdom wouldn't like being left in the dark.

It was a surprise, but I'm sure they had a reason for it. Preparations or not, a year was a long time.

We left the inn and walked down the block to the

transportation depot. People openly stared and whispered, but I did my best to ignore them, instead focusing on Mitchell and what clues he could give me about the palace.

"Can you tell me what kinds of things I will be doing? Or are you sworn to secrecy?" I asked, hoping for answers but not wanting him to get in trouble. I didn't want to win the prince, but knowing a thing or two about what to expect would help settle my nerves.

"There are a lot of courtship items planned, of course. Like dates so the prince can get to know everyone, but some of the items chosen by the Curse Breaking Committee are on the more physical side. Nothing too intense, but there is combat training."

The color drained from my face. "Why will I need to know that?" I asked, my voice an octave too high.

Does holding five-hundred page books count as exercise?

"My condolences," he said and nodded solemnly, understanding how dire that option was of the bunch, but he didn't elaborate further.

I couldn't help but laugh at the ridiculousness of this situation. I, the most antisocial and least skilled woman in this town, was being asked to flirt with the prince and somehow solve the curse while learning combat moves? I didn't consider myself horribly self-deprecating, but I was a realist, and this was something I was ill-equipped for.

He joined in on the laughter after a minute. If it weren't so depressing, I'd be offended, but at least we both were on the same page.

The carriage was far larger than I expected and painted in a deep black. There was gold filigree and detailing along the edges, with intricate carvings adorning the exterior. It was grand by all standards, especially when compared to the creaking wood I was used to seeing.

"I'll get the horses from the stables," Mitchell said as he took my hand to help me into the carriage. "Get comfortable, we have a long ride ahead."

The inside was just as opulent, with fluffy thick cushions that were more comfortable than anything else I had sat on. I smiled as I got settled, petting the cushion as if it were a pet. Maybe being in the palace wouldn't be so bad. Noticing a throw blanket in the corner, I picked it up and wrapped it around myself, kicking off my shoes and stretching out.

For a few minutes, I was able to relax and forget it all, forget that I was about to embark on something that was wildly out of my control. The idea was fleeting.

Reaching into my pocket, I pulled out the prophecy

again, rereading it so many times that I almost had it memorized.

The part about the marriage seemed clear.

Befalling the trials
of love's stead
The Summer Maiden
learns the truth of the dead
with the second-born prince
enthralled and newly wed.

Trials could be the contest. But then later in the prophecy it said *for all and for each other, for one loves the other*.

Does that mean only one person is in love in the marriage? If the prince is enthralled, then it implies his bride isn't. My mind turned over the phrasing. For one loves the other... Yet, they did it for all *and* each other. Maybe the prince and his wife will be friends, but he'll be the only one in love.

Left with more questions than answers, I settled in for the ride. Mitchell led the horses as I watched a world go by that I'd never seen before. In all my thousand and twenty-four years, I had lived in Everbrook, never to leave, and now I had the sinking feeling that I'd never see it again.

CHAPTER FOUR

Hours later, we were coming up the drive to the castle just as the sun was beginning to set. Tall torches and bonfires were lit as we made our way up the drive, attendants moving between them with their own handheld torches. Guards opened the gates when Mitchell approached, calling my attention to the castle instead of the flames. Two other carriages just like ours were ahead of us, arriving only moments before.

It seemed I wasn't the only one that wanted a head start.

Mitchell opened the door for me and extended his hand. I took it and hopped out of the carriage inelegantly. Picking up my bag, he led me up the steps.

From the first carriage, a tall woman in red exited. With how her fabric moved, it appeared thick and expensive. She stared up at the castle gleefully, a wide smile on her face, until she looked around and saw me and the other carriage. Her eyes narrowed. She had dark black hair that cascaded down her back in gentle waves and pale white skin. It was as if she had no blood in her veins, for her skin held no flush or imperfection of any kind. Picking up her skirts, the woman turned her head and walked up to the entrance, set on being the first through the doors. Her royal representative ran to keep up behind her, nearly tripping on luggage to keep up.

The second carriage guest was opposite in nearly every way. She too had black hair, but it was cut bluntly into a short bob right below her ears and perfectly straight. She was slightly more filled out and shorter than the tall guest. Her long dress was a soft pink, her complexion umber, and the sleeves and neckline of her dress covered all available skin. Only her hands and head were visible. Surveying her surroundings, the pink-dressed guest smiled when she saw me.

Smiling back, I introduced myself. "Hi, I'm Madeline."

"Eliza, a pleasure to meet you," the woman in pink said.

We walked together up the steps to the castle entrance, Mitchell and Eliza's representative walking behind us. Two immense wooden doors, easily over twenty feet tall, were before us. They had thick iron bands to reinforce the oak planks. In the center of each was a large door knocker, one a lion, the other a bear. Mitchell moved forward and lifted the handle of the bear to knock. The sound echoed loudly, as if the inside of the palace was an empty void.

"And you are?" Eliza asked the woman in red once we all stood beside each other.

"Eudora," she said as she looked us up and down, assessing her competition.

How would I be able to keep track of the names of thirty women? When they all arrived, it would be impossible. I looked between the two, trying to commit their names to memory with rhymes.

Eliza is kind-a, Eudora thinks I'm a fool-a.

I snickered to myself.

Eudora's head snapped back to me. "Something *funny?*"

It only made me laugh harder, which was a negative point in my self-preservation skills. Once I got a hold of myself, I shrugged and said, "Life is certainly funny, Eudora. It makes a fool of us all. I'm Madeline, by the way."

Before she could analyze me further, the large door before us opened with a groan. Four palace attendants greeted us. One stood ahead of them, implying her seniority. Her brown curly hair was pinned in a bun, but several strands lay framing her face. They complimented her hazel eyes.

"Hello, Victoria," Mitchell said to the woman. "We have a few of our potential Curse Breakers here early. Can you show them to their rooms?"

Victoria nodded to him and asked for our names, pausing an extra millisecond after Eliza to refer to the list on her clipboard. Ushering us in, she said they'd direct us to our rooms.

We followed her for a few feet before I stopped, noting our representatives still behind us. I addressed mine, not wanting to ignore his help.

"Mitchell, thank you for getting me here safely. Will I see you again soon?" I asked.

"Of course you will, Madeline. It was great to meet you," he said with a warm smile. "I'll see you every day."

"Good," I said with a nod. He must be involved in the competition somehow.

Running back to Victoria, we continued down along the quiet palace.

"This is the Curse Breaker Hall, Wing A," Victoria said. "You three are located here, coincidentally, but we have two wings to house all contestants. There are fifteen per hall."

The hallway stretched out long and regal, polished

marble shining under the warm glow of the candle sconces. Fifteen cream-colored doors lined the hall, seven on each side and one at the end. The doors had markings on them that looked like lace overlays, but as I walked closer, I could see they were actually wood-burned designs in delicate strokes. Each was a little different from the last, with different blossoms and vines woven in.

"You will all meet the royal family at dinner in three hours. We know you have had a long journey, so we will have the staff bring up snacks shortly. We may have a few more guests arriving tonight, but this first dinner will be smaller since we aren't expecting everyone until tomorrow," the man beside Victoria explained, before turning to coordinate with the other attendants.

"How wonderful and lucky we are to get to meet the royal family tonight in a more intimate setting," Eliza whispered to me quietly.

I was not looking forward to meeting anyone else, at any time, but at least this first night would be a smaller group.

"If you need anything at all, there is a cord beside your door and your bed. If you pull it, it will ring your designated staff and they will come to your room," Victoria said, bringing us to a stop in front of one of the doors.

"Thank the stars for that," Eudora exclaimed, clearly used to being served. Victoria stared at her for a beat, letting the silence linger pointedly, before continuing.

"There are clothes and other items you may need already in your rooms. Please change for dinner. The closets are organized by occasion. Curse Breaker Eliza, this room is yours," Victoria said.

"Thank you." Eliza dipped her head at each of us in farewell, opened her door, and went in without looking back.

"Eudora, this way," Victoria said, gesturing for her to follow.

While I waited, I closed my eyes, focusing on my breath. I let the surroundings fall away, including Eudora's shrill voice complaining about something in her room. It had been a whirlwind of a day, with so much out of my control, and I needed that quiet.

When I came back into my awareness and opened my eyes again, I flinched in surprise, seeing Victoria standing studying me.

When she didn't say anything, I mumbled, "Sorry, I'm a little nervous. I'm not used to attention."

"Not a problem, Curse Breaker Madeline. You'll have three hours to rest in silence now," Victoria said. It was kind, but also hollow, like she was placating a child.

"That sounds great," I said with a sigh, grateful regardless. The tightness in my chest loosened in relief.

"This is your room here," she said, steering me to another spot in the hall.

Glancing around, I noted there were no names on any of the doors. "You've memorized the rooms of all thirty contestants?" I asked. "That's a lot of work."

"It's my job to remember," she told me. And judging by how Mitchell and the other servants, attendants, or representatives—not sure what everyone was technically called—moved around her, she had earned the respect of her position.

Now that it was my turn, I stood in front of the door, scared to go through it. Distractedly, I looked at the pyrography again. It must have taken a great deal of time to do.

"It's beautiful," I told Victoria, glancing back. "The artist is really talented."

"It was me," Victoria said with a smile. "Thank you."

"Really?" I gasped, one hand pressed to my chest. "You did such a good job."

Victoria explained with her hands, gesturing at the door. "It was Prince Dredrick's idea. He knew I was a wood burner and wanted his brother's potential brides to be surrounded by art."

"That's very kind of him," I said, turning the knob

and opening the door. "They must have a very loving relationship."

Distracted by the view, I didn't register her reply. The room was just as stunning inside, with several paintings on all four walls, each featuring a warm-toned sunset. In the corner nearest the bed, a stone fireplace stood ready, with a vase of yellow flowers on the mantel. The bed was closed off with sheer white curtains. I got to stay *here*? The only thing missing was shelving, then it would be perfect.

"You are staying in the Orange Sunset Room," Victoria said, walking to the center of the room and pointing out some accents. "All of the rooms have different themes based on the sky. Some have rain scenes, pink sunrises, twilight, midnight, afternoon sun, storms, evening snow, you name it."

My wide eyes fell in love with the room. Maybe this adventure wouldn't be as bad as I thought. "It's the most lovely place I've ever seen. Did you paint these too?" I asked.

She laughed. "No, I'm just a wood burner. But the painter does live here as a permanent resident. We like to change up what paintings we feature every decade, so they have consistent work."

I never imagined what the castle would be like, not

until now. Thinking of the royal family as patrons of the arts had never crossed my mind.

"Thank you, Victoria, I'll be happily resting now," I said, the distractions of the art settling and my tiredness seeping in. "How will I know where to go for dinner?"

"I'll be back to escort you in three hours. Don't forget to change," Victoria reminded. With the soft click of the door closing, she was gone.

I pushed back the bed curtain and sat on the comforter, energy waning from the stress of the day. Before any other coherent thoughts could form, I kicked off my shoes and laid down. Seconds later, my eyes closed.

A knock on the door jolted me awake, heart hammering in my chest. Disoriented, I looked around me, wiping the drool off my face. The candles were low, the room darker than it was seconds before.

"Madeline, it's time to go to dinner," Victoria said through the door.

Shit. I jumped out of bed and opened the door, hair flying behind me with the current of air.

Victoria took in my startled face and asked dryly, "Overslept?"

"Yes," I said with a grimace. Eudora scoffed. Glancing over Victoria's shoulder, I saw her and Eliza looking perfectly put together in even finer dresses than they came in with. Eliza's dress was high-necked and long-sleeved again. It was impressive that the palace took our preferences into account when buying our clothes.

With a sigh, Victoria scolded, "I'm going to walk them to dinner, and I'll send someone back for you, okay? You have ten minutes, so hurry it up."

"On it," I said and closed the door before she even turned away, running around the room.

"Closet, closet." Muttering to myself, I turned in a circle. "Aha!" Throwing it open, there was a bright room full of outfits for all occasions. Most of them were in light colors of creams, yellows, and soft pinks, but there were a few jewel tones scattered about.

With no time to waste, I pulled out a stunning blue dress. It seemed fancy enough to meet the queen, so I threw it on without thought, leaving my travel dress on the floor of the closet, and rushed to the bathroom in search of a hairbrush.

Finding it, I ran it through my hair, catching a few snags. I snarled at myself in the mirror. This is *not* how I wanted to make my first impression.

Sooner than I'd like, a knock sounded, signaling my

time was up. "Coming," I yelled, exiting the bathroom and throwing open the door for a second time. Distractedly, I walked forward while bent down, tugging on my shoes.

Hitting a solid wall of chest, I stumbled back. Before I could fall on my ass, a large hand grabbed me by the waist.

"In a hurry?" the gruff voice asked, righting me so we were face to face.

I looked into the soulful green eyes of the heir to the kingdom and squeaked, "Yes."

CHAPTER FIVE

His laughter sent butterflies across my chest. I don't know why people talk about butterflies being in their stomach, that's not where mine lived.

"I'm so sorry, Your Highness," I said in a whisper, recognizing the prince from his official portraits. "I didn't mean to walk into you like that."

"There is nothing to be sorry for, Madeline. You may call me Dre," he said, his charming smile lighting up the hallway. He stood tall with wide shoulders and filled-out arms, taking up all the space in my small view. I'd always thought Prince Dredrick looked stiff and sad in the royal paintings, but in person he seemed full of life with his chiseled jaw and kind green eyes. He had blonde hair trimmed short, but it was more of a golden caramel than his portraits.

He was damn alluring. I hadn't dated anyone in a long time, by choice, but that didn't mean I was immune to attraction. "You know my name?" I asked, thinking I might pass out.

"Of course. When Victoria told me you were running late, I volunteered to escort you," he said, as if it were normal for royalty to run errands or do favors for staff and guests. He pushed back his hair with a swoop.

"Not Prince Reignold?" I asked and then slammed a hand over my mouth in embarrassment. "Not that I'm ungrateful, of course," I added behind my hand. The blush covering my cheeks grew until I was sure that I was a red tomato standing in a dress rather than a human. I may not want to honor the goddess of love, but the deity of lust? Vexion occasionally tickled my days.

I was here in a competition for Prince Reignold, technically, so meeting his brother first was a little odd.

"He is busy with the other guests. We've had more early arrivals than we expected," he explained, offering his arm to me.

He graciously did not mention my status as a red vegetable. Or were tomatoes fruits?

Gulping, I threaded my arm through his, and he led me down the opulent hall. My steps echoed, but not as loud as my heartbeat.

"Victoria told me you commissioned her work on the

doors. Thank you, they are beautiful," I said, feeling jittery in the silence. I imagined that each door had to have taken a week or more, and there were thirty of us.

"She is very talented," he said. "Are you a fan of the arts?"

I nodded emphatically. "I mostly focus on books, but anyone that can use their creativity to make something from scratch is amazing to me."

"I agree," he said, looking down at me. "I wish I had that skill."

My arm subconsciously tightened in his, bringing us a half-inch closer.

"Art makes life worth living, don't you think? I was curious who of my brother's hopefuls would also appreciate such an important part of life," he said, the phrasing so similar to how Victoria explained it.

Oh, it was a test. And apparently I passed? I felt prideful for a moment, beaming up at him as he smiled back. Catching myself, I looked down at my feet. The hypocrisy of my lonely heart. I'm not here to win or impress princes, I reminded myself. I need to be average, boring, and sneak under the radar so I can help and then leave.

For a few minutes, we walked quietly down the hall. Stress sweat trailed down the small of my back, sticking to my dress. We must be almost there.

"Everything alright?" the prince I'm not supposed to blush over, asked.

"This is a lot of pressure," I admitted, staring at the closed door he led me to.

He turned me to face him, lifting my chin with a finger. "Everything in life is," Prince Dredrick said. "Here, you just have to be yourself. If it's you in the prophecy, nothing you do or don't do will matter. It's you or it isn't. There is no pressure in that, at least. You can't mess up a prophecy."

"That's true," I whispered, searching his face. "But it's probably not me."

He smirked. "Maybe yes, maybe no."

Prince Dredrick's finger trailed down my neck before he stepped back, clearing his throat. "Let's go in, shall we?"

I pressed my lips together and looked down, eyes welling.

"Hey, it'll be alright," he said, leaning down to put his face in my view.

The crown prince of Riversend was crouching before me. It felt illegal for a prince to do such a thing.

With a laugh, I wiped my face. "Right. I can do this." Taking a few deep breaths, I centered myself and looked into his eyes.

"You will walk in there with your head held high," he said, staring back just as intently.

His voice sent a shiver down my spine. Thrilled that he believed in me, I wanted to give him the satisfaction of being right. Prince Dredrick believed I could do this, so I could.

Nodding, I took his offered arm, and he pushed open the door to the dining room. Sound and light greeted us, and it took a minute for my eyes to adjust.

The supposedly intimate dinner for the early arrivals felt like anything but. Before us were two long tables, one table at the end and perpendicular to the other, set above on a dais.

"Madeline, how *lovely* of you to join us," the woman in the middle of the dais said. Her emphasis could only be taken as sarcasm. I recognized her immediately, our Queen Arika Komari.

With dark brown curly hair framing her face, a petite stature that her son did not inherit, and eyes that seemed impossibly large, she seemed doe-like, despite her blue eyes staring at me in challenge. Her necklace was crooked on her chest, a large blue gem that matched those doe eyes. It looked heavy.

"I apologize for being late," I said, curtsying. Glancing back at Prince Dredrick, I added, "I'm so grateful to Your Highness for showing me the way here. I would have gotten lost without him."

"Yes, thank you, brother, for bringing Madeline to the festivities," a third voice added. I turned and met the eyes of who I was supposed to be fighting for, Prince Reignold, surrounded by five women in finery. Eliza and Eudora were there, as well as three others that must have arrived during my nap.

"Found her for you, *brother*," Prince Dredrick said to him, a teasing tone that felt more charged than necessary.

His eyes narrowed, jaw tense. "Like I said, thank you."

Breaking the tension, I addressed the man I was supposed to be here for. "Prince Reignold," I said, dipping into another curtsy. Unfortunately, I wobbled a little on the way back up.

In the portraits, Reignold was always slightly behind Dredrick, showing his standing. He seemed shorter than the heir in the portraits, with softer features and fewer muscles. But in person, it was clear they diminished him on purpose. No, he wasn't the muscular heir to the throne, but he was strong and lean. Reignold had brown eyes and his hair was also a deep brown. Other than his eyes, he looked more like his mother than his brother did.

Prince Reignold dipped his head with a small smile that didn't reach his eyes. But something lingered in his stare when they shifted to his brother and I.

In a matter of seconds, the dynamic felt clear. One prince was grounded, neutral but powerful, while the other was bright and colorful, visible to all, like a rainbow.

I wasn't worth the jealousy, but just as Prince Dredrick instructed, I kept my head up with a confidence I was not used to.

"Thank you again, Prince Dredrick," I said and stepped away. Taking in the tables, I paused. Was there etiquette to seating arrangements that I should know? I'll have to start reading that book on royal traditions tonight, so I wouldn't feel so lost.

"I've saved you a seat, Madeline," Eliza said with a small wave.

With a grateful smile, I walked along the long table to sit beside her. As the only one dressed in a jewel-tone, the rest in black, I stood out like a sore thumb. Victoria had said just to pick a dress from the closet, but maybe I was supposed to use a certain one.

Prince Dredrick smiled to his brother and moved on, coming to a seat beside his mother. They spoke softly as a servant prepared a plate for him.

"We were going around the table getting to know

each other," Prince Reignold said to me, leaning over from his seat to include me in the conversation. "Why don't you share a little about yourself?"

I blushed as all eyes turned to me, ducking my head. "There isn't much to say, I'm afraid. I work in a bakery and spend my time reading."

The silence was thick, waiting for more. Unused to socializing, I opened my mouth to stutter an apology for being awkward when a voice cut through.

"And who have you lost?" one of the new people asked.

Startled by the invasive question, I barked, "Why?"

"We all have lost someone, to true death, right before the curse started," Eliza explained beside me. "It's part of the criteria we match in the prophecy."

"Where does it say that?" I asked.

"*Entwined in stolen grief,*" Lyra explained, after introducing herself.

"Oh," I replied. I hadn't realized what that meant before the curse, but it made sense. "Both of my parents, the day before the Ageless Blight. I'm an orphan."

Eliza nodded. "My cousin."

"My father," Eudora said.

"Sister," Lyra added.

"My sister as well," said the person beside her. I

didn't catch her name. They reached for each other, squeezing their hands in solidarity.

The third looked away, not divulging who they lost. No one pressed her on it.

"I wish this wasn't something we all had to experience. Death isn't easy, whether it's forever or unending. I too lost my father shortly before the Ageless Blight. It hurts to know he could have been with us but passed at the wrong time," the prince said after a moment. He stood and lifted his glass. "A toast to those not with us."

Reaching for the cup, I raised my glass with them. I hadn't noticed it before, taking a tentative sniff to guess its contents. It held a plum liquid, possibly wine. I took a sip when everyone else did, confirming it was indeed an alcohol I did not like.

When I put my glass down, I noticed Eliza doing the same beside me. In close proximity to her, I noticed a detail I had previously missed. The hand holding the glass had burn scars wrapping up to her wrist. Surreptitiously taking in her appearance, I wondered if her choice to cover up had more to do with scars than it did with a preference for modesty. She also must have re-spritzed her perfume before coming down to eat. The floral scent suited her, though it was strong. There was a balance to it, some sort of tangy note undercutting the honeysuckle.

It was none of my business to focus so much on her scars, so I turned my focus instead on studying Prince Reignold with the other women. They seemed to get along well enough, talking between each bite of food. I didn't bother interjecting, even if I had something to say. I wasn't here for the prince. Instead, I needed to focus on the women. Who was meant to be the winner? I needed to figure that out so I could help them instead.

Other than Eudora, everyone seemed nice enough so far. Time would tell who may be the best fit.

Every few minutes, my eyes drifted to Prince Dredrick on the dais.

And he was often staring back.

We were just wrapping up our three-course meal when the doors swung open with a boom. I jumped in my chair, giving a startled yell.

A twinkling laugh bounced across the room, and a stunning woman in a black evening dress (*I definitely missed a memo*) with ice blonde hair walked across the hall like it was hers alone. On her hand was a sparkling gold diamond ring. "Sorry I'm late, darling," she said. She paused, seeing us seated at the long tables. "How lovely, they are beginning to arrive."

Prince Dredrick looked up and smiled at the intruder. My heart sank. While she and Prince Dredrick both had blond hair, she was snow, and he was the sun.

Right, he had a betrothed. How could I have forgotten that? Prince Dredrick and Serena had been engaged for the past century. The Crown called her Princess Serena, even though they weren't yet married. Maybe that was part of her betrothal agreement. I remembered there had been parties across the kingdom for weeks, thinking this was a good sign for our future. Why hadn't they gotten married yet?

"I'm so glad you could grace us with your presence, love," Prince Dredrick responded. He stood up, kissing her cheek and pulling out the chair beside him.

I wiped the damning expression from my face and looked down.

Eliza dropped a hand onto mine and squeezed.

"Sorry, I'm fine." I lied through my teeth. "The sound started me, and I may be getting a stomachache. I'm not used to such large meals."

"Of course," Eliza said with a smirk. "I would be happy to eat your dessert for you."

I laughed, glad someone was sharing a joke with me.

"Hey, I didn't say that was necessary," I joked back, pulling my hand away and grabbing my fork. "Chocolate makes everything better."

"I agree with that statement," Prince Reignold interrupted. Addressing the other three women, he said, "Excuse me, ladies."

The prince stood and walked to our side of the table, sitting beside me. His close presence seemed to pull all the air from the room.

"What's your favorite dessert, Your Highness?" Eliza asked.

His response was muffled. Blood rushed to my ears, drowning out any sound. I quickly scooped up some of the cake and shoved it in my mouth, chewing as my body calmed down.

In the past hour, two attractive princes have been very close to my person, and I reacted. What have I gotten myself into? I'm supposed to keep a low profile.

"Are you alright, Madeline?" Prince Reignold asked.

I looked up from my cake, already two bites in. My face was that of a chipmunk. "Yes," I said with my mouth full. Pointing at the cake, I mumbled, "Compliments to the chef."

The prince laughed. "I'll be sure to let him know how enamored you were by it."

Blushing, I ducked my head again. This was going to be much harder than I thought.

CHAPTER SIX

Prince Reignold remained with us for the rest of the meal.

My eyes drifted to Prince Dredrick and his fiancée. Their laughter with the queen was hard to ignore. Shouldn't the queen have given some sort of speech? Helped us feel welcome? Maybe it would come tomorrow, when all the other contestants were here for this weird game. Or I could have missed it, I reasoned. I was late, after all. Her silence toward us seemed odd when one of the women here could join her family.

When the queen left the table to retire for the night, we all stood to curtsy. This seemed to signal the end of our evening, finally.

"Can you wait a moment, Madeline?" Prince Reignold asked when I stood to follow Eliza.

The other contestants looked behind them as they filed out, wondering why I had the pleasure of alone time with the prince. Eudora fixed me with a glare when she thought no one was looking.

Nearly everyone noticed.

"Sleep well. Tomorrow we'll have much to talk about," Prince Reignold called to them. The women curtsied as they said their goodbyes, led out of the hall and back to their rooms.

"Good night, dear Madeline," Prince Dredrick said as he and his fiancée left. She smiled at me, dazzling and unbothered.

Sitting back down, I glanced at the second in line to the throne. He repositioned his chair at an angle to face me. I awkwardly mirrored his movements, cringing when the chair legs scraped the floor and echoed in the cavernous room.

Servers blew out torches on their way out, leaving us in the low amber light of the candles on our table.

"What did you need, Your Highness?" I asked nervously.

"I wanted to thank you for being here," he said, looking down at his hands. He had a little dimple on the left side of his face. I stared at it before thinking through the words.

That was what he wanted to say? It was simple and oddly adorable that he wanted to tell me that privately.

"It is my duty, Your Highness. I was summoned, and it is my honor to comply," I said awkwardly. If I admitted to not wanting to be here, would that count as treason?

The prince picked up on my reluctance. "It feels like there is something you've left unvoiced in that response," he said. "You can be honest with me."

"It's the truth. I'm glad to be here," I said with a tight smile.

His raised brow told me he did not believe it. "It's alright if you don't want to be here. Hell, I don't want to be here either."

"You don't?" I asked, shocked by his admission. Wouldn't any man like to have thirty women competing to marry him?

"Being a prince is not something I'd wish on anyone. Don't get me wrong, there are benefits, and I've enjoyed many of the privileges, but the pressure is unexplainable. Forever, I'll be someone obligated to do what is best for everyone but myself. I'll never escape that." He shrugged. "And then having a prophecy tell you this is your only chance at love? If I mess this up, I'll be alone forever, dooming myself and the kingdom. I'd be the cursed one, responsible for it all from this moment forward."

I hadn't considered that perspective, and it broke my heart. The loneliness of it, knowing this prophecy and not being able to do a thing about it or risk the lives of thousands... it wasn't a great way to live. Even if he tried to deny the prophecy's validity, that was a threat to himself. The Komari family was given reign over the kingdom because of prophecies, after all. Long ago, they were foretold to lead us into safety and prosperity. And for many generations before the Ageless Blight, they had.

"You're right, that sounds difficult. More than I thought it would be, honestly. Thank you for opening up about how you feel. It couldn't have been easy," I said, regretting my snap judgement.

If he could be that honest with me, then I could be too. "The letter I received said I had to come or be charged with treason."

His brow furrowed. "The notice said that? Can I see it?" he asked, voice rising an octave.

"Yes, Your Highness. I can bring it to you tomorrow," I said.

"Would you mind terribly if I see it tonight? When we're done talking, I can walk you to your room," he said. He seemed distressed by this news. Did he not have any oversight over that part of the process?

"Of course, Your Highness," I said with a bob.

He flinched again. "You can call me Reign."

I laughed. "Your brother also asked to not be called his title. Why don't you like it?"

"It's so formal," he said sheepishly. "I already feel like I'm separated from everyday life. Being called my title makes it worse."

When he put it that way, how could I refuse?

"Reign," I said, testing it out. It was an appropriate nickname. "Okay. In private, I'll call you Reign. I don't want to get in trouble in public if the queen hears me call you anything but your title."

His answering smile beamed, the dimple more pronounced as his bright white teeth lit up my vision. His eyes even twinkled, seeming genuinely happy. I couldn't help but smile back.

"Thank you, Madeline. Even if it was upon penalty of permanent death, I'm glad you are here. From just these few hours, I feel like we have a lot in common. Especially in how we feel about all this attention. I hate it as much as you do."

"Oh god, is it noticeable that I'd rather be reading in bed than talking to people?" I cringed and hid my face.

Reign gently pulled my hands down, holding them.

"No, you just seem shy. But so am I, so it's nice. I'd love to be friends. We can help each other get through this together?" He phrased it like a question, thumb caressing the top of my hand.

I inhaled deeply, my hand tingling where he touched it. "Just friends? Are you okay with that?" This was supposed to be a competition to get a wife and save the kingdom.

"You just admitted that if the penalty wasn't death, you wouldn't be here. I think that means you aren't interested, at best." Reign grinned like it was a joke, but there was vulnerability hidden in his expression.

"No, you have it wrong," I rushed to say, shaking my head.

"You do want to date me?" His eyebrow raised, hope shining in his eyes.

"No," I said apologetically. "Not that you aren't attractive, you really are one of the most beautiful men I've ever seen, but I don't want to be royalty."

That sounded wrong. What the hell am I doing?

The room grew darker, shadows casting on his face. "It's not all it's cracked up to be, that's true. What am I wrong about then, if not our potential relationship?"

"Yes, I hesitated because of the treason charges. I even considered running, but I knew I would always wonder. Not about being a princess, but if I could help the kingdom. That's why I'm here. The children..." My voice cracked. "I have this neighbor, Flora. She's been two, for a thousand years—" I choked up, unable to continue.

His expression tightened. "I know. What's happening to them isn't right."

Nodding, I added, "I would have come to see if I could help children like her, even without the warning. If I can be of any use to you in solving this curse, you can count on me, okay?"

Reign's smile returned, and it lit up something in me too.

"I'm going to love being friends with you, Madeline," he said. "Now, since we both like reading, what's your favorite Apes Matthews?"

We talked until the candles on our table burned low, going over our theories and what could happen in the next book. There were several paths it could take, and we each guessed a different one. We had a few months until the sequel came out. Maybe the curse would be over by then and I'd be back to my usual life.

I supposed we'd have to be pen pals, writing letters back and forth with our reactions, when the time came. I found myself looking forward to it.

A cough sounded at the door and I squeaked again,

my heart jumping out of my chest. Victoria asked if I needed help getting back to my room.

Reign laughed beside me and stood, extending a hand. "You startle easily."

Taking his hand, I rose from the table. "I'm not used to being around so many people. I've felt like a scared bunny all day."

"I'll help you get settled then, little bunny," Reign said with a smile, then paused. "No, bunny doesn't suit you. How about mouse? Sprout? Baby?"

I blushed and his smile grew.

"Baby it is. Mind if I call you baby, Madeline?" He offered his elbow, so similar to how his brother did. Walking with him, Reign dismissed Victoria and led me down the hall.

Why did he have to be so cute and nice? And why did being called *baby* cause such a reaction in me? Was I that starved for affection? "I don't think the other contestants will like it if you call me baby."

"That's not a no, though," he noted with a smirk.

"It wouldn't be appropriate," I said instead of denying, tucking my hair behind my ears.

"Then it'll be just for special occasions," he amended, before thankfully switching the subject as we reached the hall and I gestured to which door was mine.

He held the knob, staring at the engraving on the wood for a beat before speaking.

"There will be a lot of people here tomorrow. The rest of the contestants will arrive overnight or before breakfast."

"Are you nervous?" I asked.

"Deathly," he admitted.

I took his hands in mine, gripping them in front of me, feeling their warmth. "We'll get through it. Together, okay? Us shy folk have to team up."

"Thank you," he whispered, pulling me into a hug. "It means more than you know."

We breathed together, my head tucked into his chest. It had been a long time since I had a friend, but I understood friends didn't usually hug for this long. Yet, I felt safe in a way that I hadn't in years. Nothing in the world would have made me pull back first.

A minute later, he sighed and let me go. I went into my room to get the letter from my bedside table. Handing it to him, he pocketed it without looking. His eyes took in what sliver of my room he could see from behind me before we bid each other goodnight. Watching him walk down the hall, something hopeful settled over me.

It would be nice to have a friend, someone with whom I could confide my deepest fears. And somehow, in those short hours, I felt like he could be that for me. Eliza was turning into a friend too, of course, but there was something about Reign. I felt protected with him. Not only that, I felt like I could protect him too. *Equals.*

My earlier impressions of the prophecy came back to me. It said *for all and for each other,* but for *one loves the other.* Would it be us, the married friends?

If I became his friend, was I putting myself further down a path I did not want?

No. There were many women here. He would make more friends. And there was another interpretation to consider, a forced marriage would fit the prophecy just as well. But that wasn't a positive end for Prince Reignold, and the Crown would never publish something that could make them look bad.

All prophecies had multiple possibilities. If I continued to work through each problem strategically, I could help the children and escape back to my normal quiet life unscathed. I'd prove Hester wrong, come back to her and her granddaughter, and we'd start our lives again.

Staying ahead was the only option. And I reasoned I couldn't do that if I stayed in the background.

There was another way to see it. There had to be.

CHAPTER SEVEN

Waking to what seemed like a dozen voices outside my door, I groaned. *It was too early for all this noise.* Turning over, I covered my head with my pillow, closing my eyes again.

Bangs sounded in the distance, interrupting my fitful sleep, and a far away voice called out, "Time for breakfast, get up!"

Damn, I did not want to miss any of the delicious food.

Dragging myself out of bed, I brushed my hair and looked more closely at my clothing options. When I got dressed last night, I was flustered and in a rush. Sure, I was also flustered and rushed right now too, but by the sounds of it, so were many others, and I had some time to sort it out. There were over two dozen outfits, by my quick counting. One side had outfits labeled for particular occasions, the other had no labels. I glanced at the labeled side, finding one that said "day one."

It was a pantsuit in all black. I hated pants. Glancing back at the rest of the outfits, around ninety percent of them were dresses, thank the fates. Though the other pants outfits looked like they were for athletic needs. I'm sure I'd fail whatever test that was. Beside the day one outfit and some of the athletic wear, there were a few other black outfits, but it was a dress with a sparkling see-through layer on top that stood out. It was like they were stars. The outfit was labeled "Curse Breaker Ball."

I hoped I didn't have to dance.

Fists hit my door in quick succession. "Ten minute warning!" the voice called.

Swearing, I pulled on the pantsuit, swiped on a bit of makeup left in the bathroom, and walked out into the noise.

"Breakfast will be served in the plaza, after going through some announcements. Be ready to go!" a familiar voice said at the end of the hall.

Turning toward it, I found Mitchell and smiled widely. He held a clipboard loosely to his chest.

I wove through the crowd to reach him, watching as he answered questions from the women clamoring around the space. There were only supposed to be fifteen people in our hall, but with everyone crowded together and staff weaving between them, it felt like more. Every outfit was the same in the sea, with hair and skin and body types of all kinds in between.

"Hello again, Madeline. How was your first night?" He smiled, seeming happy to see me again. It was nice.

"Enlightening," I decided to say, unsure how to put it. I could barely believe all that happened in a short time. "Overwhelming," I added after a beat.

Before Mitchell could respond, my view was blocked.

"Will we meet the prince today?" A trim woman I hadn't met yet came forward, stepping in front of me. I narrowed my eyes at the back of her head and moved aside.

"The prince will preside over this activity, of course," Mitchell said, though I noted a coldness that wasn't there when he spoke to me.

"But will we get to *meet* him?" she pressed again, talking with her hands.

"Like I already said, Rosamund, everyone will get time with the prince," Mitchell said, with less patience this time.

Eudora walked by at that precise moment. "Some

more than others. And with both of the princes," she said with a glare.

"What do you mean?" Rosamund asked, trailing after her.

Stopping a few feet away, Eudora sneered, "Madeline here snagged time with both of the princes, alone, in one night. Seems against the rules, if I say so myself."

It took all my effort not to roll my eyes. It's not like I schemed for those events to happen. It was purely accidental.

"Enlightening and overwhelming, you say?" Mitchell asked me in a stage whisper before turning to the two other hopefuls. "It's not against the rules. If the prince, or both in this case, want to talk to a potential Curse Breaker, *at any time*, then they can. The removal of the curse is the most important task there is, wouldn't you agree? They have to isolate who the princess is, and quickly. You wouldn't want to *interfere* with the Crown saving the kingdom, would you?"

Eudora fumed, her eyes narrowing and jaw clenching as she looked between me and Mitchell.

The smirk grew on my face before I remembered to school my expression. Damn, Mitchell was good at this.

"We're leaving, anyone still in their rooms won't get to meet the prince," Mitchell yelled down the hall, turning away from Eudora. A burst of women stumbled from their rooms at the warning, adjusting their hair.

There were so many people. Crowding, anxious, excited, all wanting to be the one to win the heart of the prince and save their world. I didn't fit in with them, not at all. Being a princess was the farthest thing from what I wanted. With that many eyes on the royal family, their decisions were not purely their own.

I lined up where Mitchell told me to, noting the growing whispers. Peeking behind me at the other women, I noted Eudora yapping to the people beside her. They, in turn, would whisper to those in front and behind them. In moments, the majority of the women in Curse Breaker Hall, Wing A were staring back at me.

"Excuse me," a soft voice said, cutting in line to be behind me. There was some discord, but not enough to deter her from changing spots. I smelled the floral tang I was starting to recognize and turned, finding Eliza. My shoulders relaxed and I smiled at her.

"I hope you slept well, Eliza," I said.

"I did, and you?"

"The beds are so comfortable here that I didn't want to wake up," I said sheepishly, not bringing up how my mind was spinning. "I'm not used to luxury."

"It does take time getting used to it, but soon it will feel normal," she assured me.

Curious, I wondered about her life before this. Her statement made me think she had a similar experience, going from nothing to everything. Living over a thousand years meant there was always so much history to a person. You could know someone for decades and not even know a drop of their experiences.

Victoria rang a bell at the end of the line before walking forward to stand beside Mitchell. As we left the hall in single file, the second set of doors on the opposite end opened and another line of women joined us with their two attendants. Our single file line turned into walking in pairs, Curse Breaker Hall, Wings A and B coming together. It felt like a march, our shoes clicking the floor in unison.

But a march to what?

CHAPTER EIGHT

We arrived at what Mitchell called the plaza a few minutes later. It was a U-shaped patio off to the back of the palace, separated and yet part of the structure at the same time. There were ancient trees shading the space and a podium where four people stood in similar black uniforms, but with white sashes across them. The patio was paved with smooth, cream-colored flagstones, with white chairs set upon them.

Following the attendants to the chairs, we sat in rows, an aisle separating us into two sections. I was separated from Eliza in the shuffle and sat between the two girls that lost their sisters. Forgetting their names, I asked, and they introduced themselves as Lyra and Kieran, but stared awkwardly at each other from either side of me, so I took the hint and stood up so one of them could take my spot. Once they were seated with each other, I sat back down in the spot they left and sighed.

Kieran don't want to see ya, and Lyra will never be ya, I said to myself. Only twenty-five other names to learn.

"Settle down, settle down," one of the sashed men said. "We will begin in just a moment."

As I settled into my new seat, I couldn't help but notice the excited chatter that filled the air. The gathered women seemed eager to learn more about what was to come, their voices rising and falling in anticipation. I didn't share the same excitement, despite wanting to help.

"My name is Rowan, head of the Curse Breaking Committee. Myself and my peers work with the palace's trusted prophet to interpret their visions and how the Four, our deities of age, death, love, and lust, may react to them. You are all gathered here in the palace for two important reasons—" he paused, emphasizing the last sentence, "to discover who among you will break the curse and bring back the god of age, and to marry Prince Reignold, pleasing the goddess of love. Thank you for being here." Rowan started clapping, nodding emphatically at the rest of the committee at the same time.

The women followed suit, clapping for themselves and for each other. I mimicked them, feeling very awkward about it, like I was in a choreographed performance and wasn't briefed on the steps.

"We have identified certain markers from the prophecy and other insights that led us to choosing you, the thirty women among us. Some of those markers may be obvious, while others may be subtle. Do not question why someone is here or instigate fights. You are all important to the fate of our kingdom," Rowan explained with a pinched expression. "By bringing you together, you are all now part of the makeup of the curse's demise. It could become an accumulation of multiple women engaging with the prince that creates a chain reaction and breaks it, rather than just one woman. While only one will win the heart of our prince in the end, that does not mean multiple women will not play a part in the events."

If Rowan intended to be encouraging, I begrudgingly admitted it was working. A moment ago, I felt lost among the people so happy to be here. But saying we all had a part did help, in a way.

"You will all stay here for at least one month, so the prince can get to know you. After that, he will eliminate all but five final potential brides. After that, you will be brought into the Crown's trust, learning more about the Ageless Blight. Regardless of who goes or stays, you are all part of our history now, to be known as Curse Breakers."

Rowan paused, letting us take in his proclamation. Based on how the murmuring increased around me, he was right to wait. This direction seemed to have distressed a few contestants. But why? Five left out of thirty did seem extreme, but the chance of winning was already low. And now, they'd have a month to prove themselves. All hope didn't die if they made a bad first impression.

My guilt over this competition lessened. I could stay one month, help Reign, and then he'd send me home with his matches already chosen. I'd have done my part for the kingdom and helped my new friend, and then he'd have an easier dating experience once the second month of the competition hit. It was a win-win.

After the murmurs died down, Rowan added, "Don't be worried, Curse Breakers. This means you have more of an opportunity to prove yourself to the prince. While you all will have an impact on the removal of the Ageless Blight, this is still a competition to find love, and there can only be one winner for the prince's heart. We will continue to treat it as such. Starting right now, in fact. Our future queen, Princess Serena, is our first guest. She is here today to give advice about dating a prince, having successfully wooed one of her own. Everyone, welcome our future sovereign."

He angled his body to the side and motioned to the right. We stood and clapped, turning to where Rowan aimed our attention. From the top of the stairs, leading down to the plaza, the elegant Serena stood in a gown of silver, matching her hair. A delicate circlet was atop her head. She glided down the stairs and gently curtsied when she reached the front of the room.

Why did she have to be so perfect?

When she rose up, she put her hands together, cooing at us, "One of you will be my new sister."

Lyra and Kieran glanced at each other, eyes bright.

"Rowan has asked me to talk about what it's like to be betrothed to a prince, as well as tips for dating one. I know this situation is not how most people would have expected to meet the love of their life, but it is a unique opportunity to give back to our kingdom. Thank you for being here."

Can everyone *stop* saying that? We were forced here. Sure, most of these women felt happy about it, and I wanted to help too, but it was still a forced endeavor. I glanced around, checking if anyone else had an outward reaction that clued me into their thoughts, but I found nothing.

"I would say my first tip is to understand the

perspective of our princes," she said, walking around the podium. "They are beloved, but very isolated, because of who they were raised to be and the responsibility that entails."

How was she raised before coming here? Where in the kingdom did she come from? Another reminder for me to look at my royal biography.

"It takes time for a prince to open up and even longer for them to feel understood," she continued. "You need to be patient with these boys and don't expect too much from them. The kingdom's expectations of them are already too much to bear."

Was her advice to lower our expectations? I understood what she meant about feeling misunderstood, but the rest felt placating and disrespectful. I squinted my eyes at Serena, disliking her even more.

Someone raised their hand.

"Please introduce yourself as you ask your question," Serena instructed, gesturing to her.

"My name is Amelia, from Trent. How did you make the prince choose you out of everyone in the kingdom? What qualities do royalty admire?" she asked. She had a kind tenor to her voice. It was soft but not meek, although the question felt manipulative.

I should keep an eye on her. You can't make anyone do anything, not in any long lasting way, if they didn't want to do it in the first place, but it looked like she was willing to try.

"There was no making of anything, Curse Breaker Amelia. It started very casually. My family was visiting the palace to discuss some matters with the queen, and we got along. I came on every visit after, begging my parents to stay for more extended periods so that we could spend time together. It was a friendship before it was romantic," she said, causing many in the crowd to sigh.

"Then, it grew into more. We found common ground. Prince Dredrick and I have a lot of similar beliefs about the kingdom, which is important to his position. It will be for Prince Reignold as well. Dred and I do not have children as of yet. But, if anything should happen to us before we had children, then Prince Reignold would be the king next. He needs to know *you* see policy the same way, or have at least the spirit to solve problems with him. Even if he never becomes king, he will be heavily involved in the royal family his whole life. Show the prince what matters to you and it might match up. Royalty favors honesty and compromise."

Eudora stood up next, her hair braided down her back today. It made her long neck even more apparent.

"My name is Eudora. Pleasure to meet you," she said, skipping where she was from. "My question is, why haven't you two gotten married yet? Is there something we can do when we get engaged to speed up the engagement period?"

A few of the women gasped at the question, but Princess Serena lifted a hand to calm the murmuring. "Don't fault her for asking. I'm sure most of you were also thinking it, weren't you?" She surveyed the room with a raised brow and many people nodded, admitting they held the same wonder.

She stared at Eudora, taking stock in her unabashedly. Eudora did not cower to it, like I would have.

"With the Ageless Blight still in effect, we decided to wait. Pledging to be with each other until death do us part seemed tacky when death couldn't actually part us," she said and chuckled at her attempt at a joke. "Now that we have the prophecy, we've started planning for life after the Ageless Blight. The future we've been waiting for is upon us, thanks to you all."

She clapped for us and in a swell, the crowd clapped with her. They seemed like they glowed with hope and determination, while I couldn't shake the feeling that had settled in the pit of my stomach. Serena meant to be inspiring and helpful, but it felt hollow to my ears. I forced a smile and followed along for what felt like the dozenth time in under an hour, keeping the discomfort off of my face.

Her saccharine-sweet voice set me on edge.

"I think that is enough questions for now. There will be many more opportunities to meet with Princess Serena," Rowan assured. "Thank you, Princess Serena and Curse Breakers."

"Thank you all for being here. I can't wait to get to know you. Good luck with your first dates." Serena went back up the stairs on quiet feet, as if her shoes were made of clouds.

"Now, for today's challenge, each of you will have ten minutes to speak to Prince Reignold and give your first impression. The person who stands out the most will be rewarded with a private date with the prince tonight. Don't worry if you don't win today's challenge, as you will still have time with the prince tomorrow at the Curse Breaker Ball. Before then, any other questions I can address about the competition?" Rowan asked, searching the room.

Ignoring the panic at his mention of a ball, I shot up before anyone else could and introduced myself, asking Rowan, "Madeline, from Everbrook. How exactly do we end the Ageless Blight with the prince?"

Rowan's lips pursed, as if he hoped that no one would actually ask about it. "When the competition eventually narrows, the final five will meet with the creator of the prophecy to discuss it further. They will be able to answer more questions on why Thailor, the god of age, has forsaken the kingdom. There are a few factors we are keeping secret for everyone's safety, including the name of the prophet. As is tradition with the ruling family, their prophets are protected. Those that remain will be sworn to secrecy."

Nodding, I plopped back into my seat. At least there was a plan, but I wouldn't be around to see it.

"How long do we have to prepare until we talk to the prince? When does it start?" Eudora asked next.

"It starts now, Eudora," Prince Reignold said from behind me.

Startled, I turned to see him leaning against a door I hadn't noticed. He seemed relaxed, his hands in his pockets as he kicked off the door and strode down the aisle that separated the chairs. After speaking to him for so long last night, seeing him vulnerable and shy, I thought he would act the same way here.

But no, this was the prince mask. The cool, calm, and collected man that was born into a role.

He reached the podium, standing in front of it as he surveyed all the women that were just told to expect less of him. Did he hear that too?

The rest of the women seemed to fall away as I

watched him, mesmerized by how he could shut out the noise to meet his duty. The overeager didn't matter, the snooty were ignored, it was like I was the only one here, watching the prince play his role. For a moment, our eyes met, and I swore I saw a flicker of the real Reignold behind the mask.

He was trapped in this situation, just as much as we were, but he had his whole life to find himself in the puzzle, while we were new pieces thrown in.

"Sorry to startle you all," he said with a grin. "It's the first day, and I imagine we are all a little on edge. That's why I wanted to take this time to spend a few minutes with all of you. I know ten minutes isn't much time, but there will be more time for us as these weeks go on. It's an icebreaker, I suppose." He shrugged sheepishly and pushed back his hair. "Can I ask a favor of my Curse Breakers?"

"Of course," I said, staring him straight in the eye. Other affirmations sounded around me.

His gaze sought mine, as if he could hear me over the other voices. "I'd appreciate your patience as I get to know all of you. Being a prince looks different on the outside than the inside. Princess Serena was right, it will take me a while to open up."

So he did hear her. That's awkward.

"I might slip up, forget someone's name even," Reign

said, breaking eye contact to laugh and look around the room. They accepted his comment as a joke, though I knew he was serious, remembering all thirty women would take time.

Focusing back on me, he added, "Madeline, could I borrow you first?"

Chairs scraped as people turned to stare at me. I ignored the whispers that sprung from his request, but the prince didn't.

"Is there a problem, Curse Breakers?" he asked, expression fixed on me.

Eudora stood up and said, "Your Highness, me and the other Curse Breakers were discussing this morning how Madeline has already had time with both you and Prince Dredrick when no one else has. It feels unfair for her to go first when she has already met you."

His eyes moved from mine to stare down Eudora. "I would like to point out that I also spent time with you, Eudora. Everyone that arrived early had time with me. Yes, I spoke longer with Madeline. Do you want to tell me what to do on our first day together? I think I need to get to know my potential bride for longer than a day before I let them tell me what to do, don't you?" The sharpness in his voice was unmistakable. Eudora struck a chord.

Eudora's confident demeanor faltered under the

prince's gaze, her cheeks flushing in embarrassment. How in the world did she think challenging the prince publicly, on the first day, would help?

"Rowan and the committee decided we should keep all of you for a month, but I want to make it clear that *I made no such promise*," the prince said to the room. "If I unequivocally know that someone is not suited for me, I will send them home, at any time, prophecy or no prophecy. You understand me, Eudora?"

I bit my lip to keep from smiling and stood up from my chair. Across the aisle, Eudora said, "Of course, I'm sorry. Please forgive me, Your Highness."

"Ready, Madeline?" Prince Reignold asked, not acknowledging Eudora's apology. He stepped away from the podium and extended his hand to mine.

"Ready," I affirmed as our fingers intertwined, a dark glee filling my chest.

<h1 style="text-align:center">CHAPTER NINE</h1>

He led me out of the plaza, hand still in mine. It was warm and steady, anchoring me.

We didn't speak for a time, instead feeling comfortable just being with each other. Was it really so easy to be comfortable with him, after only one night?

The large thick trees that had semi-circled the plaza thinned out, and on the other side was a garden of pink roses, with smatterings of delicate willow trees, benches, and fountains between them. The space was filled with the sounds of fountains and birds. It was a little oasis, just off the chaos of dozens of women that were surely now talking about us.

"That was impressive," I said, speaking first. "You can command a room."

"Thanks," Prince Reignold said, "my heart feels like

it's going to fall out of my chest, but I imagine it might be like that all day."

"Maybe," I admitted. "It's a lot of pressure, this experience, but I wanted to let you know as your friend, that you did well back there. Good first impression."

"That means a lot, thank you Madeline." He smiled. "I'm glad we talked yesterday and decided to be friends. I could certainly use one in this."

The prince led me to the bench in the center of the garden, tucked under the largest willow tree. Sitting together, my hand still in his, we enjoyed the quiet, cocooned in safety, being ourselves in a way we couldn't while in public.

The flowing branches of the willow swayed gently in the breeze, filtering the light that reached us so we were shadowed from the sun's rays. I took a deep breath, inhaling the scent of the roses, before speaking. "You probably shouldn't call on me too often. At least not publicly," I said. "Our friendship is already very noticeable."

Even in the line this morning, I could feel the animosity rolling off of the other Curse Breakers.

He looked at me from the corner of his eye. "What if I want our friendship to be noticeable? Why would I hide a friend?"

"With the way this competition is set up, us

spending time together and being called first too often would upset people. They'd see me as a threat, taking away from the time they should spend with you. It'll make things harder for me when you are not around," I explained, nervous about the possibility of being singled out more.

"Harder how?" he asked, his hand gripping mine tighter.

"Like what happened right now with Eudora. Gossiping, bullying, isolation, maybe even pranks—that kind of thing." I shrugged as if it wasn't a big deal, when it was. "They don't know we already decided not to date. They'll assume I'm the person to beat."

He angled his body to mine and I matched him, turning away from the soothing garden and focusing on his face.

"I don't want you to get hurt or punished for our friendship. I'll try and make it less obvious, but I will not stay away from you if I need you. Promise you'll do the same if you need me," Prince Reignold said, eyes searching mine.

For all and for each other, for one loves the other, whispered in my ear.

Nodding mutely, I blocked the thoughts out. It was ridiculous to think something as innocent as friendship would lead me to a crown.

"Who do you think I should go on the date with tonight?" Prince Reignold asked, changing the subject. "Is there anyone that stands out to you?"

"Out of the Curse Breakers I've met so far," I said, saying our new designation, "Eliza feels the most like a princess to me. She is kind and considerate. She also isn't aggressive to me even though she knows just as well as the others that I've had more time with you. This morning, she sought me out for company while others pushed me away."

"That's good. I'll take her then," he said softly, his thumb grazing over the top of my hand. "Though I don't like hearing that people were already discourteous to you."

I ignored the second part and carried on, hoping he would drop it. "You should decide after you talk to all of them. I've only met a few people so far, but you should also trust your judgement. Maybe someone else will be better, but Eliza's who I like the most so far." I didn't want to overstep my bounds like Eudora.

"I'm sure once I meet everyone, I'll agree with you about Eliza," Reignold said. "But I'll keep an open mind, thank you."

"How are you feeling about it all?" A rose petal dropped from the bush in front of us, pulling my eyes from him.

"Overwhelmed," Reignold admitted. "I didn't like that Eudora spoke about you like that. I appreciate boldness and confidence, it balances what I have trouble with, but that was a firm stance to take at the beginning of this. It made me feel like I was already losing control."

I tried not to feel righteous about a prince defending me but failed.

"I'm sure this was an isolated incident," I assured him. "Why not send her away then? You know it won't be her in the end, so don't waste your time, like you said." There was no reality where Reignold would marry Eudora, I was sure of it.

"Part of that was saving face, unfortunately." He cringed. "I have the power to send people away, of course, but I'm going to try not to for this first month and stick to the plan. If she listens to what I said, she can stay, she deserves a chance to meet the boundary I set." Reignold sighed. "I've unfortunately learned that when you let public ridicule go, it spreads. You have to address it head on. She deserves a chance to make up for it."

I agreed with his logic but still pouted. I'd have loved to never see her again. "Okay, I guess you are right."

"Don't worry, *baby*," he said teasingly, hand cupping my face. "Like you said, she won't be the one I marry."

Leaning into his hand, I smiled and took comfort in

his touch. When was the last time anyone touched me like this? Truthfully, I couldn't remember. "I'm so grateful to have you as a friend. I haven't had one in so long."

"Me too," he said, searching my eyes and pulling back. "Now if you'll excuse me, I believe our ten minutes are up, and I have twenty-nine more speed dates to get through."

"What a busy prince you are," I joked, knocking his shoulder as we stood and walked back to the path. "It's so beautiful here. I'd love to come back and explore it more with you, when you have the time."

"We should," he agreed, stopping by a rose bush. "We've selectively grown the roses over generations until they lost their thorns, which is helpful for the gardeners—" He plucked a rose from the bush, handing it to me. "—and when we gift them."

I accepted it, inspecting the thornless stem and the pink bloom. "Don't let your guard down just because it is de-thorned," I said. "When you lose one way to defend yourself, you get creative."

"I'll keep that in mind," he said as we reentered the plaza. The quiet bubble we were in fell away when faced with the other Curse Breakers. As one, they all turned from twhere they stood talking in clusters, seeing me and my gifted rose.

I curtsied to the prince and walked to the back of the room. He called for Eliza next. When she returned a few minutes later, she told me they had a lovely time and that she had a good feeling about it. I was happy for her. I felt like she could be a good medium ground between someone shy while also being good with people. A prince would need someone like that.

The next few hours were long, especially with so few people willing to talk to me. I've spent as much of them with Eliza as I could, but she often took time to mingle and get to know the rest of the group as well. Nibbling on the breakfast they served while women waited for their turn, I watched her work.

By lunch everyone had their time with the prince, and Eliza was announced as the winner of the dinner date. I clapped a little too hard for her, earning a few stares, but I paid them no mind. She'd make a great princess, the prophecy *had* to be about her.

CHAPTER TEN

After Prince Reignold—no, *Reign*, I reminded myself, getting used to what he told me to call him—left with Eliza, there was very little of interest for me at the supposed welcome dinner that night. Yes, it was a feast, so the food was distracting for a time, but it was not welcoming in the slightest. Other than quick greetings, I didn't speak to any of the other Curse Breakers, and they didn't invite me into their conversations either. When things died down, I was the first to leave after the queen and Princess Serena. Prince Dredrick was not in attendance.

Making a quick stop by my room to pick up my book on the royal family, I followed the directions Victoria gave me to get to the library.

A few corridors away from the dining room, up a

grand staircase with red velvet steps, was my destination. I was shaking with anticipation as I pushed through the heavy doors, the red carpet continuing into the space, minimizing the sounds of my steps. The library was large, it may even be bigger than the entirety of the main street in Everbrook.

Books lined every corner, with dozens of sections and shelves. They were organized with five-digit numbers instead of signs for each category. A quick stop at the librarian's counter and I was on my way with the number for the history and prophecies section.

The scent of old parchment hung in the air, mingled with faint hints of lavender and something metallic. A few sconces flickered on the far wall, but the main sources of light came from the chandeliers and the fireplaces.

I wondered, how often did they need to replace these books in the thousand years since the Ageless Blight came to be?

Picking up books of interest, I found a few on Reversend's past before the curse, on telling the future, and even some on prophecy analysis. I was running out of space in my arms, having to balance the books with my chin, when I paused my browsing to find a table.

Glancing around, I spotted a cozy corner near one of the fireplaces. As I made my way toward the table, I tripped. The books tumbled, one slipping from my grasp as my body lurched off balance. Before I could drop another, I was caught by something solid. With a gasp, I righted myself and recognized the strong arms bracing me.

"We've got to stop meeting like this," Prince Dredrick said with a wide smile.

My face flushed red as I apologized. "I'm so sorry, Your Highness."

"Don't be. I'm glad to see you again so soon. It's not like we have much opportunity to talk at meal times," he commented, leaning down to pick up my dropped book. "Ah, *The Surprising Results of Prophecy* by T. C. Wilder. Competition research?"

He led me the few remaining feet to the table, hand on my elbow.

"Yes," I replied. "I thought it would be a good idea to study completed prophecies. I heard this book shows what they thought would happen, and then what actually came true. It seemed like a good one to study, since I was picked based on a prophecy." I stood by the chair, arranging my books as I talked. I put my personal book to the side, its cover more worn than the ones I picked out. *Princes are supposed to sit first, right?* You never know with royal etiquette.

"And you didn't want to ask the Curse Breaking

Committee about why you were chosen?" he asked, taking the seat across from where I stood.

I'd thought about it, of course. "I assumed they'd be biased, having worked on it for so many years already. Plus, I like doing things myself and approaching a project with fresh eyes. If I had their opinion first, I may miss some things," I said, pulling out my chair now that he had.

He smiled. "That's a good idea. Let me know what you find. As you've said, I've looked at it for too many years. I can't be objective about it either."

Years. That was confirmation the Crown had the prophecy longer than they said.

Prince Dredrick leaned forward, his elbows resting on the table as he studied the titles of the books I had selected. "You have a keen eye for research, Madeline. These are excellent choices. I prefer nonfiction to fiction. Despite my love for the arts, I've never been interested in novels. I prefer the way the world is interpreted in paint rather than words."

There was a flutter in my chest, warmth spreading at the praise. I had always been a learner. It was like both princes held part of my personality, one holding my love for fiction, and the other that felt the joy of knowledge.

I traced the edge of a book with my fingertips,

glancing at the two stacked beside him. "What did you pick to read today, Your Highness?"

"How many times have I told you to call me Dre?" he asked instead of answering.

"Only once, Your Highness," I said with a grin. I liked how playful he was, so different from how I felt most of the time. Something about him made me want to play back.

"Consider this my second and final time then, dear Madeline. I'd like to be on less formal terms with my potential in-laws," he said, his eyes twinkling with mischief. He reached out, gently tucking a stray strand of hair behind my ear, his touch sending a shiver down my spine.

"Okay, Dre, I'll try to remember that," I said, laughing inside. The brothers were a lot alike.

The prince glanced around the library, as if ensuring we were alone, before leaning in closer, his voice lowering to a conspiratorial whisper. "Between you and me, I've always believed that the key to understanding the true nature of the prophecy is to be paranoid."

"Paranoid?" I asked, not sure what he meant.

"*Always question your theory.* Never accept your first answer as fact. Give two, three, even four possible meanings to each line," he explained.

I found myself drawn in by his words, my own voice dropping to match his tone. "That's a good concept, Your—Dre," I corrected myself. "There's something about the prophecy that feels... incomplete. As if there are pieces of the puzzle still missing."

Prince Dredrick's smile widened, a spark of excitement in his gaze. "Exactly."

We settled into a comfortable silence, each of us engrossed in our chosen texts. I found my gaze drifting to his more than I should admit. He would furrow his brow as he read, switching back and forth to the index as he referenced different sections in the large tome he read.

I glanced at the clock, realizing it had been hours.

He followed my gaze. "He's probably done with his date now."

"Yeah, probably," I said, hesitating. I hoped it went well with Eliza.

"Don't worry, Madeline, no one can outshine you, from what I've seen," he said, misinterpreting my tone.

"What?" I startled, looking back at him. "No, I'm not worried about that."

"I like confidence in a woman," he said with a laugh, leaning back in his chair.

"No, no, nothing like that. I'm not here to m—" As

soon as the words were out of my mouth, I realized my mistake.

I repositioned the books around the table, hoping he wouldn't call out my almost slip up. His eyes followed my hands, mouth opening to question me when he spotted the weather-worn book.

"What's that?" he asked, reaching for my copy.

"I brought it from home. I thought having a book on royal family traditions and history would be helpful," I admitted, embarrassed.

"This looks like a really old copy," he commented, thumbing the spine and turning to the copyright page. His eyes scanned, looking for the date.

I shrugged. "Yeah, I know there have been updated editions since then, but I don't know, I don't like getting rid of books." I also didn't want to tell him that I hadn't bothered to buy the updated edition, because I didn't feel like learning more about them at the time.

He flipped the pages, stopping on an old family portrait before shutting the book quickly. "It wasn't written by an approved palace correspondent. I wouldn't consider everything you read in here as fact." Dre crossed his arms and leaned forward, pushing the book aside. "But you do have me, after all. I'll answer any questions you have." He smiled devilishly, winking.

I smiled, lost in his green eyes. "You are right about that."

"What's your first question?"

Thinking of our awkward shuffle earlier in the evening, I asked, "Am I allowed to sit down before you sit down?"

He barked a laugh. "Really? That's your first question?"

"Well, it was topical. I stood around like an idiot for a minute, not sure if you should sit first or not." My face was flushed.

Shaking his head, he said, "No, it's not an official rule. I'd still advise it during public settings, but in private ones, no. Some people might care, but I don't."

I smiled. "Good to know."

"How about we strike a deal?"

Intriguing. Who would have thought I would have multiple deals with royalty. "What kind of deal?"

"I'll be your royal tutor. You can ask me anything you want, as long as *I* can ask you questions whenever I want too." He tapped my hand on the table.

The deal seemed uneven to me, like I was getting all the benefits. "What would you want to know that only I could tell you?"

"Plenty of things," he whispered, eyes trailing along my arm, up my chest, to my face.

Was it my imagination, or did this engaged prince think I was attractive? I certainly thought he did, but thinking it and acting on it were entirely different matters.

Hesitantly, I said, "Okay."

"My turn, then, since you asked about seating." His eyes seemed to sparkle as he asked, "Why don't you want to break the curse and marry my brother?"

My breath caught. Every denial I could say vanished, as if I didn't know the words. Was he teasing or digging? Maybe both.

I am in over my head.

CHAPTER ELEVEN

My heart sank. "I had hoped you didn't catch that mess up," I said with a sigh. "Of course I want to break the curse, I just—" I hesitated again, catching myself. It was easy to be comfortable with him, but I couldn't forget that he was the heir of Riversend.

Anything I said out of line could lead to a treason charge.

"Please, be honest," he said, voice heavy.

Looking up, I studied him. The red of the fire seemed to glow around his face. Despite the fire, I was chilled, worried even. He seemed open—was it too good to be true that he could be a friend to me too? It was like it was meant to be, meeting him, talking to him... our paths were meant to cross.

"You can trust me," he added.

Something zinged in my heart.

A shiver running down my spine, I found myself leaning closer.

"You are right. I don't want to marry your brother," I admitted in a hushed whisper, feeling emboldened. How could I be having this conversation back to back, with both brothers, so soon?

The heir to the throne laughed lightly. "Well, you are putting in a lot of effort for someone that doesn't want to marry him," he said with a flourish to all the books.

Taking a risk, I shook my head. "We came to an arrangement. I told him that I would help him win and choose his bride. I really do want to help the kingdom. But when it's done, I just want to go home. All this attention is a lot to me."

He considered me for a moment. "That's very brave of you, to lay it all out like that with my brother."

Shrugging, I said, "I just want to help the kingdom. I'm sure many other people would do the same."

His smile was thin. "No, Madeline, many people wouldn't choose the kingdom over themselves. Don't deny your bravery."

"Thank you," I said softly, my voice barely above a whisper. I wasn't used to compliments.

Just yesterday, talking to a prince so informally would have been horrifying, but now I was spending time with two princes in private. Joking with them. He glanced around before speaking. "Can I tell you a secret? It's been weighing on me and since you trusted me, I thought..." His voice trailed off.

"Of course. I promise I won't tell anyone," I said, taking it seriously that he would trust me like that.

"Myself and Serena are also in an arrangement," he told me.

"What kind of arrangement? An arranged marriage?" I asked slowly, not sure what he could mean. She had seemed like a perfect future queen, from our short interactions. Other than that one part of her advice, that is. Maybe it wasn't a love match after all...

"No, like you and Reign. We're friends. We aren't going to get married when the Ageless Blight is solved."

So the reason Serena gave for their long engagement was a lie. Interesting.

"Oh," I said, momentarily stunned. "Can I ask why? You could have anyone you want, why pretend to be off the market?"

I tried not to let my mind go wild with that thought. Just because he was technically single, doesn't mean I could pursue anything. If I was not willing to date the spare because of the attention that came with it, being involved with the heir was completely off the table.

"Well, not *anyone*," he said. "But I needed to pick someone so the kingdom could feel like life was still moving on. Serena had her own reasons for wanting the title, so we came to an agreement. We're friends. I'm grateful we've had each other during this time."

How could he not have all the options in the world? He was funny, considerate, incredibly attractive, liked to study—*oh*. I shouldn't go down this path. It wasn't my business to speculate, and just like with Reign, there was a lot I didn't know about being royalty.

"Thank you for sharing that with me, Dre. It must have been hard to keep a secret that big for all these years. Does your family know?" I asked, talking to the apparently *single* heir to the throne that was sitting close to me in a dark, romantic library. The prince I wasn't supposed to like, I tried to remind myself. It was as if this information awoke Vexion in me, taking all my clear judgement away.

"Yes, Reign and my mom know, but we don't talk about it much. In royal families, a lot goes unsaid. Being royal is like being alone in a crowded room, every day of your life," he explained.

"I would say that sounds lonely, to not really know each other, but I wouldn't know. I've been alone this whole time, alone in empty rooms instead of crowded ones." Shrugging, I acted like it wasn't a big deal, but he saw through it. You can't really miss what you've never had, not in the way people who have lost it all have. I barely remember my parents now. Some days that loss felt so big, and other days it's like it never happened.

"You've had no one?" he asked quietly.

"My parents died in an accident the day before the curse. I had no siblings, only a few relationships here and there, but nothing serious. It's just been me," I said, explaining to him what I shared with Eliza and Reignold the night before.

"I'm sorry, sweet Madeline. I'm sorry for all of it," he said, in that guilty way that only someone with too much responsibility could say.

"Don't be ridiculous. You didn't start the curse, and we've all gotten used to it after a while. As you know, you can get used to anything, even curses and forsaken gods, if it lingers for enough time."

"Yeah," he said, eyes going off to a faraway look. He scratched at his collar and glanced at the clock again. "I should get going."

He stood up, gathering his books, and I bid him a good night.

"Dre, wait," I said, jumping out of my chair before he could get too far.

He turned around. "Yes?"

I walked up to him, nervous, but wanting to return the favor. "You're brave too," I said.

His eyes watered for a moment before it pulled back, as if nothing had happened. "And you're dangerous."

I stiffened. "What?"

He chuckled, the sound deep and warm, reverberating in his chest. "I mean that as a compliment. A woman who questions things? Who doesn't accept the convenient answer given to her? Who goes out of her way to make other people feel brave too? That's a rare trait." He walked closer to me, a breath away. "Be careful, Madeline. Not everyone in this castle appreciates people who think for themselves."

My stomach tightened at the warning. "Do you?"

His smirk softened into something more thoughtful. "I do. I'll see you at the ball tomorrow."

The air between us shifted, something tense but not unpleasant settling between our words. Before I could overthink it, he turned, telling me good night.

"Good night, Dre," I replied, seconds too late, his form too far away to hear me.

Despite my reservations, the insistence that he was *not* for me—that no one here was—it hurt to watch him walk away.

Retreating to my room two hours later, I was grateful I had memorized the way in only two short days.

How had the direction of my life changed so much? I felt like I was tilting on an axis.

Taking a few books from the library, not wanting to carry the entire group with me, I wrote down the names of the books I hadn't checked out. Dropping my haul on the vanity, next to the single rose in a vase from Prince Reignold, I got ready to sleep, scrubbing my face and quickly braiding my hair.

Laying in bed thinking about the prophecy, and *not* the prince I spent the day with, I tried to find other clues.

Dre's words, that the key to understanding a prophecy was paranoia, stuck out to me.

Taking out my copy, I penned notes in the margins, adding multiple interpretations and questions where I could.

In my reading today, prophecies were called out as tricky things and often misinterpreted. There had been a few reported in our kingdom's history, including the ones that crowned the Komaris, but I'll admit not knowing much about them. Whether it was witches, prophets, or gods that ordained the Komari family to rule hadn't mattered to me before. They were in charge and knowing why wasn't important.

After a lot of frustrated reading and scribbled notes, much more stressed than I had been when I had company, I put the papers aside and laid in bed with my book from home. Flipping to a portrait of the royal family, one of the few that included the king before his death, I gazed at it. Dre looked a lot like his father, Reign more like his mom. There was an uncanniness to the portrait, something off I couldn't quite interpret.

My eyes moved to the king. I hadn't thought of the late king much either, but he was part of the prophecy too. *Stolen grief*, it had said. Something the Summer Maiden and the prince had in common.

Closing the book, I placed it in the drawer of my side table, being sure not to mix it with my library books, and blew out the candle.

Tossing and turning, I wondered how Reign's date went and if Eliza was as good for him as I hoped she would be. My friendship with the prince was new, but it felt more real than anything I'd had in my life for years. I could be wrong, but I hoped I was already helping him break this prophecy, in my own way.

Staring bleary-eyed into the darkness, I focused on my breathing, trying to calm my thoughts and get some rest. At one point it must have worked, because my eyes snapped open, my limbs leaden and my thoughts disoriented. Something had woken me. Voices—low, clipped, controlled—like people trying not to be heard, were coming from the hall.

Sitting up, I waited, trying to see if it had been just a dream. When the sound repeated, I got up, tiptoeing to the door. I leaned my ear against it and listened.

"But you can stop this. Talk to her," a soft feminine voice said. For a moment, I thought it was Eliza's. Were she and Reign arguing? Who was "her"? Knowing I probably shouldn't, I pushed open the door a crack, turning the knob slowly to avoid being heard. It wasn't open enough to see anything in the hall, just enough for sound to filter through.

Heavy shoes scuffed on the polished floor, getting closer. I couldn't hear more of the whispers, drowned out by their echoing steps.

The feet drew closer and I turned, fearful of getting caught. I ran on soft feet back to my bed and jumped under the covers, squeezing my eyes shut. I didn't dare close the door, worried the click would reveal me. The rushing of blood filled my ears, drowning out all sounds as I waited. Eventually, my heart settled, and I peeked, sure it had been at least a few minutes.

Sitting up, I looked at the door, gasping when I realized it was now fully closed. Who had been in the hall? Was it actually Eliza and she closed the door for me? What had she been arguing about? Too scared to peek into the hall again, I settled down, bringing the cover up to my chin. Sleep came an hour later, when delirium could no longer fuel my raging thoughts.

CHAPTER TWELVE

The previous night forgotten, I stood in the entrance of the sparkling ballroom, eyes wide as I took in the celestial wonder. The room had high arched ceilings painted in a deep midnight blue. The walls were draped in rich, dark velvet curtains, a deep red that looked almost black.

Each table had centerpieces, using some of the common symbols for the Four deities. A small fountain for Miran, the goddess of love. For Veyra, a vase of clear glowing beads, the souls she could take. Thailor, of course, had hourglasses. And finally, scattered among the tables, Vexion was represented with glass apples, filled with red wine.

I was jostled as more people moved forward,

walking around me and my gawking. "Sorry," I said, moving to the side as I took more in.

Every Curse Breaker was dressed in the matching black dresses with glittering fabric overlays from our closets. We were stars and galaxies. The cuts were slightly different, matching the styles of each individual woman, but they were similar enough that you couldn't tell who came from wealth and who didn't, which was their point. We all stood together as potential brides for Prince Reignold, a clean slate in the palace.

There had been no time in the plaza today. Instead, we were told to sleep in, as we'd be up longer at the ball and needed that energy. Around lunch, dozens of servants had dressed and primped our group. They brought food so we could continue to get ready, and a few of the women even had their hair dyed. I was polished with exfoliators, primed with oils, hair trimmed and styled, makeup expertly added, and not left alone for a single second. I hadn't had a chance to speak with Eliza before they started lining us up to arrive here, but I hoped we could sit together and talk once the event officially began.

Walking along the perimeter of the room, I made my way to the tables on the far left with the apple center-pieces. Sitting down, I purposefully isolated myself from the crowd, not yet seeing my friend. Hopefully soon I could busy my hands with the food. Most of the Curse Breakers were walking around the space, introducing themselves to the other guests, or talking in little clusters like they were holding court. It is what a princess would do, I'm sure, but I'm not one of those, so I did the opposite.

"It's a little early in the event to be hiding, don't you think?" a voice said from beside me. I turned, my face flushing, to find Prince Dredrick taking the seat beside me.

"The same could be said for you then," I retorted.

He shook his head. "No, there is no hiding when you are a prince. We're like magnets, see?" he said, tilting his head forward.

I followed his line of sight, finding that while I was invisible a moment ago, that was not the same now. Dozens of eyes were glancing our way and a few groups were now walking toward us.

"That's scary," I said honestly, my hands getting clammy.

"I'll spare you the horror," Dre said with a slow smile and stood.

"No, I didn't mean—" I started, worried I'd offended him after he was so nice to me the night before.

He waved my quick panic away. "It comes with the job, Madeline, and you've admitted already that you didn't want it. I won't fault you for that, but that's my lesson for now, in our royal tutoring," he said with a wink.

Dre walked backwards a few more steps before pivoting gracefully to the crowd that was clamoring to meet him. He led them a little further into the middle of the ballroom, his golden hair and outfit a beacon in the room of magentas, blacks, and blues. Dre was wrong, he wasn't a magnet. He was the sun in the center of our galaxy, of which everything revolved around.

All stares moved from me to the prince. I was alone again. Like I wanted.

"Did he give you the magnet speech?" Reign asked, stepping in view.

"Yes," I said with a laugh. "Does he always do that?"

He nodded with a twinkle in his eye. "My brother is a showman. And it's a great party trick."

"And are you magnetic as well?" I asked him in jest. He was a prince too, after all.

"This competition does grant me more magnetism, I'll admit," Reign said with a shrug, pushing back his brown hair. His voice grew softer. "But I imagine after all this is done, the attention will grow."

That made sense. Once he and his princess fulfill the prophecy, they'll be heroes. I snuck a glance around the room and saw he was right. While it wasn't as many stares as his brother, he was drawing attention. But he was looking only at me.

"How was your date with Eliza last night?" I asked.

"She seems kind," he answered, but didn't volunteer more. He took the seat opposite mine.

"That's it?" I asked. "You've got to give me more than that."

"It was a first date," he said. "Those are usually awkward. But she was nice enough that I'd like to see her again. Thank you for the recommendation."

My smile was wide in response. He was right, first dates could be weird. I'm sure their relationship will grow with time. Before I could ask more questions, he changed the subject.

"You look beautiful tonight," he said.

I glanced down at my lap, flushed. "Everyone looks beautiful. We all match."

He shook his head. "No, Madeline, you are beautiful in your own right. Don't you forget it."

"Thank you, Prince Reignold," I said.

"Reign," he corrected.

"We're not in private," I reminded him.

"And too bad for that. I have to give a speech once the queen arrives," he said, eyes flicking to the door.

"Do you ever call her mom?" I asked. Family dynamics among royals seemed strained. Not that I would know. I barely remembered my own parental dynamics.

"Only in private," he echoed me, smiling.

I couldn't keep my smile from answering him.

Trumpets sounded from the entryway, announcing the Queen of Riversend.

"That's my cue," Reign said, standing and straightening his coat. He wore silver, matching his Curse Breakers with their silver stars and galaxies, the opposite of his brother in gold.

My eyes followed him as he made it to where his mom stood at the front of the room, waiting for him. Dre was already there, waving at the crowd. I followed them, joining the semi-circle of Curse Breakers and other seemingly important people.

Queen Arika Komari matched Prince Dredrick, wearing a gold dress that looked almost like liquid. She wore a crown, however, of sparkling black. Princess Serena was not with her. Reign stood out in his cool-toned attire.

"Welcome to the first, and hopefully only, Curse Breaker Ball," Prince Reignold said. The guests applauded. "We are here to celebrate the women that have a hand in removing the Ageless Blight, bringing back the god of age, Thailor, as ordained by our prophets. As you all know, we have kept the prophets a secret through my family's reign, from the first king to now, our great Queen Arika Komari. Passing down the secrets from parent to child, our prophets help guide us down the true path. When their sight was clouded by dark magic, and the Ageless Blight came into being, they'd been working tirelessly to reconvene with fate until they came to predict the content of this scroll."

He pulled the prophecy from his inner pocket. Despite memorizing it, I drank in every word as he read it aloud to the crowd.

"We've interpreted what we could from these words and brought all of you here, those chosen to go down this path with me. One of you will end this curse and be my bride. I can't wait to get to know you." His voice softened at the end, wistful, like he meant that statement more than the rest.

Reign seemed genuine, I wouldn't have even known that he was dreading this if he hadn't told me. A few sighs sounded from the women in the room, hoping they were the ones at the end of this.

"Thank you for being here. Celebrate today, and get to know the trusted advisors and local officials we have brought here to meet you. They'll report back to me who they think should be our next princess."

Ah, I'd probably fail this test.

With a bow to his mom and brother, Reign and the

other royals walked through the room, the crowd parting in waves. Once they sat on the dais, Serena popped up in a white glittering gown. She looked like the moon of her namesake. How did I not see her before? *Hm, I guess she and Dre decided not to match.*

Soft music played by a string quartet filled the room as Rowan directed us to take a seat and have dinner before the festivities began. The seats were assigned, so I couldn't run back to my corner or speak with Eliza. Instead, I was seated at a table with Eudora and other guests I didn't know. She gainfully impressed the officials beside us, commanding their attention like I knew she could. It was irritating to see her succeed, but it's not like I could do anything about it. I kept to myself, eating the food, until the next portion of the event began.

After half an hour, the plates were cleared, and Reign went around the room asking women to dance. A few of the girls got multiple dances, like Kieran. Her smile lit her face and his seemed to match. As I watched them glide along the floor, I wondered what they were talking about, since their conversation lasted through each spin around the floor.

I turned when the man beside me tapped my shoulder, asking where I was from. He seemed fascinated by my life as a *normal* woman working in a bakery. I answered his questions until Eudora interrupted, before looking back at the dance floor.

When my eyes lifted, Reign was walking toward me. The fork I had stuffed with chocolate cake was half way to my mouth, frozen by the sight of him with his eyes solely on me.

I'd admit it now, I had been jealous. Not because I wanted to date him, of course, but I was lonely at this table and I'd have rather been with him, my friend.

Dropping the fork on my plate too loudly, I stood from my chair before he reached me.

"May I have this dance, Madeline?" Reign asked with a bow, eyes looking up at me as he bent at the hip.

Did friends usually make each other's hearts flutter?

CHAPTER THIRTEEN

"Of course," I said with a curtsy, smiling at Reign. The silk of my skirt whispered against the marble floor as I rose.

He offered his arm and I took it, my fingers brushing against the embroidery on his sleeve. In his arms, I finally felt at peace after so much jittering. "That was a great speech for someone that hates the spotlight," I said, spinning into position on the dance floor.

Likely for the sake of the competition, the song was slow, like the rest of the music from the evening. It was a lot more fun to stare at the prince holding his potential love interests close than watching people two feet apart doing awkward shuffles. Thankfully, slow dances were also easier for me. If I had to dance to some of the quick songs, I would likely fall on my ass or do something very embarrassing.

"Hating it doesn't mean I'll be bad at it," he said with a smirk. One of his hands held mine high, the other resting on my waist. "Though I am very glad it is done. I memorized it weeks ago, saying it every night." His palm was a steady anchor against the growing nerves in my stomach.

"Great job, my prince," I said. "Dedication and discipline are things every partner wants."

His eyes softened as we swayed. The music slowed even further, violins pulling long, aching notes stretching between us.

"Oh, really?" he asked.

"Really," I affirmed.

He tucked me in closer and we spun around the room, moving from one song to the next. He squeezed my waist every so often, like he just had to flex his fingers, but my mind went numb and my breath hitched.

"So are you going to tell me more about your date with Eliza?" I asked as the music changed to the next song.

"I already told you, it was nice. I enjoyed talking with her."

Rolling my eyes, I said, "That's it? That's all you've got to say?"

"I can't tell you everything about my dates, even though we're friends. I don't kiss and tell," he said, and I wasn't sure if it was meant as a joke or not.

"Oh," I said, blinking as I took in what he said. "Well, it must have gone really well if you are already kissing."

"I didn't say that, but I didn't *not* say it either," he said with a playful lilt.

Thinking of him and Eliza burned in a way that I didn't want to place. I didn't like this feeling in my chest *at all*. I had wanted this, right? For him to date everyone except for me?

"Are you scared?" I asked after the next spin. "If we are part of a prophecy, then what if you like a person who isn't meant to be the Summer Maiden, and it doesn't work out?"

Reign stared at me for a moment before answering. "I think it would be naive of me to not be scared. But at the same time, I know my convictions. If I'm meant to be with someone, but love another, I'd fight it."

The hand on my hip tightened and my breath caught. His next words were a whisper, but I felt the conviction in them. "If destiny wants to keep us apart, it will find it has an enemy in me."

Us. Him and his wife, not me. The person I promised myself I would not become. My heart hammered, feeling like his words were etched on my bones.

We didn't talk much after that, not about anything important. It might have been my imagination, but as each song bled into another, he held me tighter, until we were barely half an inch apart. It was a weighted, yet comfortable, silence. I could spend a decade spinning with him, a center point in the universe, even with his other potential wives swirling around us in their matching celestial gowns.

After a time, he swept me back to my table. With a whisper in my ear, he said, "I'll see you tomorrow, baby. Thank you for dancing with me."

His breath tickled my skin, and the lingering warmth of his hand on me left goosebumps in its wake. Before I could respond, his hands were on Eudora, and the smile he bestowed upon her was different than how he looked at me.

What is wrong with me? He was my friend. Was formal wear a magic spell that made everything more romantic?

That must be it.

Not wanting to watch them dance or be present to see if he whispered in her ear too, I took to walking around the ballroom. I was stopped a few times by citizens that were desperate to know the prospective princesses, but they soon found me boring and moved on. On my third lap around the room, I admitted to myself that Eliza was purposefully avoiding me. She hadn't let me near her, finding somewhere else to be every time I was close enough to interrupt.

She looked stunning in her fitted gown, matching my own, with the higher collar and long sleeves. We all look like little dancing night skies, doing as the royal family tells us while we orbit them as the center of our universe.

Alone, except for when the prince shines on us.

My eyes followed her as she yet again changed seats, speaking to someone else with rapt attention. I could sit next to her, corner her, but would I really want to do that when she was so clearly trying to escape me?

"I'd like to dance with you, dear Madeline," Dre said, interrupting my thoughts. He bowed before me, so similar to how his brother had.

Jumping in surprise, I put my hand to my chest at the interruption. "I'm all danced out for the night, I'm afraid." I should have left the dessert area before my third piece of cake, and now I was suffering from it and my conflicting thoughts.

"Nonsense, you would love to dance with the heir, wouldn't you?" he said, the light reflecting on his gold outfit.

My gaze shifted to behind his shoulder, finding Reign across the room, the opposite in silver. I felt the phantom touch of his hand on my waist, there only thirty minutes before. He met my eyes and glanced between me and his brother. The woman he was speaking to changed positions, blocking his view.

"I meant me," Dre said, tone sharper than before. My attention snapped back to him, like a light flickering in the dark, drawing me in. Right, two princes, yet only one could be king. Damn brother rivalries, I didn't envy the stress that must bring to their relationship. Despite the change, Dre's smile was still there, just less bright. The jealousy between them must be difficult.

Shaking my head, I shivered as a blast of cold hit me through the layers of my dress. I looked from Dre to the ballroom around us, considering.

"Alright, let's dance," I said, changing my mind. I enjoyed Dre's company. What's one more dance?

"You are a natural in the spotlight," Dre said as he led me to the dance floor.

Pausing in the center of the ballroom, I said, "I would strongly disagree with that."

We got into position, his hand to my waist, tucking me in closer to him. His hands were bigger than Reign's, and they held me tighter. I shouldn't like this either, but my brain wasn't working logically this evening.

It had been *too long* if a simple hand to the waist by two men I couldn't have was affecting me this way.

"But you are art, Madeline, you were meant to be seen and interpreted," he said, continuing the conversation I had already forgotten about.

What an odd and poetic way to put it. "And if I don't want to be art?" I asked.

"Art is made and lived. Art doesn't get a choice in that," he said as he directed me along the room. "You just are."

There were more eyes on me now than earlier with Reign. *Magnets*, Dre had said. It was true. The weight of their stares settled on me, thick and suffocating.

I lost my footing, tripping on the hem of my dress. Dre's grip pulled me up, and I fell into his chest for a second before pushing back, straightening, and resuming the dance.

"I want to have a choice," I said weakly, heart hammering. My cheeks flamed red as we spun again. Despite not knowing this particular waltz, he was able to direct me without trouble. It was easier to follow his lead than I expected. The energy of his dance felt so unlike Reign's. I was drifting with Reign, like a leaf that fell onto the surface of a pond, floating idly.

Dre was like a current, once you were trapped in it, you had to follow wherever it led.

"And yet you are here, in the middle of a plot sprung by prophets. All that we do is determined already. This dance, your trip, all *predicted*," Dre said. It wasn't clear if he was happy or not by this thought.

I shook my head. "No, if all that we do and all that we won't is already decided, then there is no point in this competition. The right person would have found their way to the prince anyway. No committee needed, right? I could leave right now and it wouldn't matter because something would find a way to keep me here if I was the one meant to marry him."

Prophecies were tricky, but if there is anything I learned from the reading I've done so far, they always won out. In the examples across history, plenty of people tried to trick the cards and make their way out of the story, before circumstances pulled them back. It didn't always match what they thought the prophecy meant, but in hindsight, the story proved out.

"Want to test that theory?" Dre asked, his voice soft. "I could walk you out and get you a carriage right now. No one would notice you were gone for a few hours. Everyone saw you trip. Is your ankle *hurt*, dear Madeline? Do you need to retire for the evening?"

He was challenging me, and part of me wanted him to. I took in his face, the line that creased in the middle of his brow when he was thinking. Was he sincere? Or did he just want to prove something to me, or to himself, about this competition?

"No," I said after a moment. The offer was tempting, but there was more I needed to do here. "I made a promise to help your brother, and I intend to keep it."

The crinkle was gone and his smile froze.

"Of course, dear Madeline. You are a good friend," he said. "I'm glad to see my brother found someone who would so steadfastly keep their word."

My mouth opened to retort, to say anything, to try and bring back the happiness that seemed to follow Dre wherever he went, but before the words could form, there was a tap on my shoulder.

Turning, Serena was waiting, positively glowing in the candlelight. "Pardon me, Madeline, can I borrow my fiancé?"

"Of course," I said and stepped back, curtsying. There was a clutching in my chest that I was beginning to recognize. The same feeling that overcame me when I saw Reign with Eudora.

But neither of them were mine to be jealous over. And anyway, Dre said he and Serena were just pretending.

Watching them glide across the room, eyes only on each other, I'd believe they were together. They were too good at acting, that was the problem. Being a royal meant you had to put on a brave face, to do what had to be done, and that involved a lot of pretending.

Without a word to anyone, I walked out of the ballroom, keeping a promise to myself that I would not look back.

In the entrance hall I faced the choice again, the one Dre was right to test me with. In one direction was Curse Breaker Hall, and the other was the way out of the palace.

I hesitated, gripping the delicate dress in too tight a hold. The texture of it grounded me as my eyes took in the door that I could take, leaving with the dress on my back and nothing else, away from the way these princes made me feel, and safe from a prophecy that could give me everything I swore I *didn't* want.

With a deep breath, I took a step toward the door, and then another, just to look outside. To walk on the steps and see how I felt in the fresh air. Yes, that's what I needed, fresh air.

My hand was on the knob, gripped to turn it, when a voice sounded behind me.

"Curse Breaker Madeline, are you alright?"

Turning around, I found Victoria leaving the hall, in the direction of our rooms.

"Yes," I called out. "Just felt a little light-headed from all the drinks and dancing."

Victoria nodded, taking in my dejected posture. "Of course, it's been a long evening. Why don't you go to bed early and I'll bring you some cold water?"

With a shuddering sigh, I rubbed my arms, letting go of the doorknob as gooseflesh covered my skin. "Thank you, Victoria. That's a good idea."

CHAPTER FOURTEEN

The Curse Breaking Committee stared back at us from the podium on day three of the competition, waiting for the thirty women to quiet down. They were ablaze with discussions about the ball the night before, while I was just tired. Couldn't we have even one day off? Did they all have to be so loud when I'd barely slept?

Rowan stepped forward. "Welcome to our next activity. The earlier speed dating led to Eliza winning the first solo dinner date with Prince Reignold, and Eudora won breakfast with the prince today after the events of the ball. Every moment is an opportunity to shine and I heard very positive things from the evening. Good show, Curse Breakers!" He paused, head leaning forward.

My clapping was a little more awkward, staring at the back of Eliza's head a few rows ahead of me, and the empty spot that would have had Eudora.

What did they talk about last night that made Reign change his impression of Eudora? Why was Eliza ignoring me?

Rowan held up a hand to signal for the end of the forced applause. "The prince has given his notes on the contestants to his brother, who is here today to judge each of you and compare those notes with Prince Reignold. Do the brothers agree on who would make the best princess? *We're going to find out.*"

He seemed delighted by the prospect, his eyes twinkling with mischief. It's probably juicy gossip for the staff. Will the princes feud over who would be a better princess?

Murmurs rippled through the crowd at this announcement. I didn't expect that Dre would be involved in the competition at all. After spending so much time with him in the library and then again dancing last night, my heart beat faster at the thought of him reading notes about me from Reign. What would Reign have said? Would Reign tell Dre about our deal, not knowing I already told him, or pretend we were actually dating like the rest of the Curse Breakers?

"They say the most important part of a marriage is

how you interact with your spouse's family. Not that I would know!" Rowan joked. "And one of you will marry into the most powerful family of all."

The weight of those words settled over the Curse Breakers. Marrying Prince Reignold wouldn't just mean becoming a princess—it would be having the queen as your mother-in-law, and helping plan the recovery of the kingdom after the Ageless Blight. It was all fun and games, until the work was brought up and soured the mood.

Being royalty was like being a parent. If it felt easy, you were doing it wrong.

"Prince Dredrick will be your next test," Rowan said, "with more intimate conversations with the queen taking place after the first month."

I leaned closer.

Rowan's expression turned stern as he continued. "You were graced with the honor of the queen's company during the welcome meal and the ball, but now you will be dining separately. If you see Your Majesty around the castle, it is important you do not disturb her. She has important work to do in preparing for the conclusion of the Ageless Blight and the return of normalcy to our society."

He paused again to stare, favoring letting the news sit in silence.

"The format today will be similar to when you first met Prince Reignold," Rowan went on, "but Prince Dredrick will talk with each of you for double the time, to be sure he has more of an idea of who you are and how you would contribute to the kingdom. We will prepare activities and refreshments for you as you wait, but no Curse Breaker may leave this area until our future sovereign has evaluated each of you."

A figure emerged from behind a nearby tree, a mischievous grin on his handsome face. "Aren't you glad to have more time with me, ladies?" Prince Dredrick asked, winking at the assembled women.

I shook my head and covered my mouth, trying not to laugh. Was that sly prince there the whole time? The idea of him sneaking behind a tree before we entered, patiently waiting while Rowan talked, was hilarious.

Dre gave a short speech, echoing what Rowan said about leaving his mom alone and how he was testing us as future royals, but with his own flair. He called Lyra first, to which she preened over. She fanned herself with her hand and curtsied deeply before following him out.

The air was thick with anticipation, and a bit of tension, as we all waited for our turn to see Prince Dredrick. Attendants came around and rearranged our rows of seats into clusters, adding small tables in between. We scattered around the perimeter of the space, waiting for them to finish adding the floral centerpieces.

"Would anyone like some refreshments?" a server asked, walking around the room.

Gratefully, I accepted a plate of delicate pastries and a cup of herbal tea, more to give myself something to do than out of actual hunger. I moved to one of the empty tables, Eliza taking a seat beside me a moment later.

I eyed her. "Talking to me now?" I asked after swallowing the flaky dessert. It stung, her rejection last night.

Eliza's face flamed and she looked down. "I'm sorry, Madeline. I didn't react well yesterday. I was upset and didn't want to talk about it."

My irritation cleared in a second, worry replacing it. "Why were you upset? Did the date go poorly?"

Why didn't Reign tell me it went badly?

"No, it went really well. That's the problem."

"Why is that a problem? Didn't you want it to go well?"

Her eyes watered, but the tears did not fall. "What I want doesn't matter. It would be impossible for him to pick me."

My brow furrowed. "You are here because he could pick you, that's the whole point. You are a potential Curse Breaker."

She shook her head, wringing her hands in her lap. "I can't explain why, it's just the truth. I'm sorry, I didn't know what to say to you, but I also don't want to lie. I wish it had just gone poorly, so I could say we didn't have chemistry, but instead I like him and can't have him."

Taking her hands in mine, I ran a thumb along the tops. "It's okay, Eliza. You are just nervous. I'm sure he liked being with you too. And it's all still early, give it time. You'll believe it could be you soon enough."

She was quiet for a moment, holding my hand. With a nod, she let go, picking up a strawberry and blinking away her tears. "Yes, of course, that must be it. I just don't want to get my hopes up."

The quick dismissal told me the opposite—there was something she wasn't telling me. Whatever it was, I'm sure it would be fine. I mean, Reign implied he could have kissed her. With her comment on chemistry, it's likely they did.

"This is all going to turn out okay, Eliza. I just know it will. We'll all get our happiness," I promised. "The Ageless Blight will end, somehow, and we'll be free."

"Yes, free," she said, picking up her plate and walking away.

I stared after her, confused by her response. My sleepy memory pulled back up the argument I heard in the hall. Was it not actually a dream, and it was Eliza and the prince? Or someone else?

A group of women had started a card game on a neighboring table, loudly discussing how hot the brother princes were. I attempted to ignore them, circling the room a few times, eating more, changing seats. I made idle talk with other contestants and eventually spoke again with Eliza, but she avoided anything related to her date the night before.

But with each passing hour, the knot in my stomach tightened. Why hadn't Dre called on me yet? Had I done something to offend him? Despite my best efforts to remain unbothered, I was incredibly *bothered*.

And it was noticeable. As each woman left and came back, gushing about the charismatic prince, there were more pointed looks shot in my direction. Heat crept up my neck as whispers mounted.

The rational part of my brain insisted that it didn't matter when I spoke to Dre—I wasn't really here to win and he knew that. Reign and I had an understanding, and I had no intention of marrying him. But the inse-cure part of me, the part that had spent a thousand years alone and yearning for connection, couldn't help feeling stung by the perception of it.

I didn't need more friends. Now I had Eliza and two princes, but to be shunned? As I waited, I kept to myself, even disengaging with Eliza after she did her sociable rounds. It would be better for her if she weren't next to me anyway. If I were being rejected, cast out even, she shouldn't be associated with me.

It was like the other Curse Breakers were thrilled with my supposed fall, as the woman who was picked first, had multiple dances with the prince, and private time with them both.

When Dre finally called on me, I'd apologize. I must have overstepped when we talked yesterday.

The sun was low in the sky when an attendant came to tell me it was my turn. I followed them out of the plaza and to the side room I'd seen all the other women go into. It was cozy, with a white tufted sofa that curved around a circular table. There was untouched food in the middle, and a relaxed prince.

Dre was reclined, his arms behind his head as if he were sunbathing, rather than interviewing potential sister-in-laws. He smiled and stood when the attendant closed the door.

"Dear Madeline, so happy to see you again," he said. "Come, sit with me." He gestured to the space beside him before sitting back down himself.

"You too," I said, trying to appear nonchalant. From his answering frown, I could tell I was failing.

"Sit, please," he insisted again, gesturing beside him.

Nibbling my lip, I nodded and sat, shuffling along the booth until I was beside him.

"You seem stiff. Are you alright?" he asked.

"Did I upset you last night, Dre?" I fiddled with my hands. "I'm sorry if I overstepped, questioning the prophecy like that."

"I don't care if you believe in prophecies or not. Why would you think that?" He pulled my face to look at him, fingers gripping my chin. "I'm not mad at you. I'm sorry you were worried."

"You called on me last," I whispered, searching his eyes. It was embarrassing that I let my insecurities win like this.

"I had my reasons for seeing you last," Dre explained, his tone earnest, "but please believe me when I say that it has nothing to do with yesterday. It was actually one of the best nights I've had in a long time."

"Oh. Me too," I whispered. Despite everything, it was fun. I'd never been much of a dancer, but there was something special about being held and twirled around a room.

"May I?" he asked, hand extended toward me.

I nodded, not sure what he wanted, but saying yes either way.

Dre took my hand in both of his, massaging the digits. I couldn't look away from the sight of our hands entwined. Did he do this with everyone else he saw today? Or... just me?

"I hate to think you were worried this whole time," he said, rubbing in between my fingers.

Melting into the seat, my head fell to the back of the sofa and eyes grew hazy. Wow, I'm touch starved.

He chuckled at my expression. "Is this a good apology?"

I nodded with a small smile, feeling a tingling along my whole body as he switched to rub my other hand.

"Can I ask you something private?" he asked.

"Of course, we're friends. You can ask me anything," I said.

"You said you don't want to be with my brother. Do you have someone waiting for you at home?" he asked, eyes trained on my hands.

"No," I answered quickly, shaking my head.

"That's good," he said slowly.

"Good?" I asked, voice hitching.

"Yes, it's good," he said, pulling up my hand and kissing my knuckles.

Anticipation and dread filled me all at once. "I said I didn't want your brother. It wasn't because of him but because of the position of princess. Being queen falls in the same category," I whispered. "I'd be horrible at it."

No matter what feelings were brooding for Dre

without my permission, a relationship between us would be doomed from the start. Becoming the queen was not on my life path.

He gently tugged me forward until we were only an inch apart. In the space between us, my heart beat so loud that I was sure he could hear it.

"I'm not proposing, dear Madeline. But I am kissing you, if you permit me."

He leaned the last inch, giving me a few seconds to pull away should I want to. *I didn't.*

As our lips touched, electricity zinged through us. Our lips were a beck and call, coming back together the second we parted. As if connected by a string of lightning, my whole body buzzed, and I shook against him, kissing him back.

Gasping, I pulled back, coming to my senses. His eyes were dark, searching.

"What does this mean?" I whispered, trembling.

"You have an agreement with my brother, to help him find his princess. How about we have an agreement too?" he asked in a low murmur, fingers trailing up my arm in a feather-light touch.

His gaze dropped to my lips, thumb grazing the inside of my wrist.

"What kind of agreement?" I managed to ask, somehow, though my brain was not working.

"We feel. Nothing serious, just some stolen moments, while we deal with the mess of this curse."

"Would that be okay with Serena?" I asked, not daring to say the *yes, yes, yes* that I wanted to scream. I'd been with other men, but those experiences felt hollow, somehow. Scratching an itch, really, while this felt like I was coming alive.

"We're just friends, you know the marriage won't actually happen. Serena and I are nothing more than that, friends with a plan," he explained, pushing my hair behind my ears.

Dre inched his head down, bringing his lips to mine again. His teeth bit my bottom lip lightly, a nibble asking me to open for him.

"Let's talk about rules," I gasped out, putting my hands on his chest before I lost all rational thought.

"Right. Good idea," he agreed. "First, secrecy, of course."

I nodded. That was a given. I did not want to lose my head to treason.

"Second, no sex. That would cross over the line, giving in to Vexion. Especially when you are not going to stay here, that temptation is too great." His voice was firm, and the rule made sense, though it did ache.

"That makes sense," I said, flushed.

He dropped his head to my shoulder and nibbled the patch of bare skin around the strap of my dress. "That doesn't mean other things can't happen, of course, but we don't want feelings to get involved." Leaning to my ear, he said softly, "And intimacy can complicate things."

The whimper that escaped my lips when he took my ear into his mouth should have embarrassed me, but I had very little conscious thought left. "Anything else?"

"Don't kiss anyone but me," he added after a moment, pulling back.

It felt like a warning, but he didn't need to give it. A shiver ran down my spine when his hand paused at the nape of my neck. He held me there softly and a deep need filled me.

I held his gaze. "Of course, I wouldn't."

"And you?" I asked, heart pounding. "Will you be kissing anyone else?"

He chuckled, shaking his head like I'd caught him. The hardness of him, obvious as he leaned into me, only added to my delirium.

"I may occasionally have to kiss Serena at royal events, but you know there is nothing between us."

While I thought he might say so, I felt a sharp pang. "Okay."

He thumbed my lip. "Now that the pesky rules are out of the way, can I go back to kissing you, little dove?"

My body was a taught bow, waiting for him. "I might die if you don't."

At my nod, he laid me down across the couch, body fitting perfectly against mine. Minutes passed with our hushed breaths and quiet moans. If a fire was between us, burning, he was the kindling I didn't want to run from.

My hips shifted unconsciously, feeling him closer to me.

"You feel what you do to me, don't you?" he asked huskily, between kisses to my collarbone.

"You're ridiculous," I told him, but I shifted again, this time purposefully. He took it as encouragement and met my over the clothes ministrations. I knew we wouldn't be intimate, he said so just moments before, but fates did I want him more than anything I've ever felt before.

"Madeline, you *like* ridiculous," he said, pulling my mouth back to his.

I showed him that I agreed as we kissed for several more minutes, our breaths coming in hot between us, chasing the high that was surging through our enduring bodies. My dress was bunched up to my waist, his clothed leg rubbing against the center of my panties.

He knew what to do, pulling moans from my body without taking us too far. I cried out under him and he egged me on until I was a puddle, staining my underwear, spent in a way I haven't felt in an age.

Vexion was the deity of lust for good reason.

A bag of loose bones, he could have done anything to me, and I would have agreed without thought.

"As much as it pains me, we should go," he said, peppering kisses along my damp skin. "It's been more than twenty-minutes now and you need to get ready for dinner." His hand trailed up my naked thigh.

Reluctantly, I opened my eyes, panting like a salivating dog. How I felt... I've never felt that wound up and relaxed at the same time before.

My hand could never.

Laying together in this tight space, the intensity of who he was, my task in this competition, these forbidden touches—and how good he was at kissing? It all combined until it was a perfect storm. Inevitable. I had no choice but to fall quickly and deeply into his embrace.

This was not what I expected to happen when I came to the palace. Kissing this man, and feeling every traitorous emotion that came my way, was the most intense moment of my life.

Nuzzling my nose against his, I asked, "Is this why you wanted me to be last?"

"You caught me," he said with a grin. "Because a few extra minutes with you was my primary goal today. I told the attendants to dismiss everyone to get ready for dinner while we talked."

I felt a lot better about waiting now. "Shouldn't your goal have been evaluating your future sister-in-law?"

"My brother can handle himself," he said, something seeming to catch in his throat.

"Everyone is gone, you said? No one is waiting for me to open that door and leave?" I said, jutting my chin to where I entered.

"That's right. No one is waiting," he said.

"Good. Can you sit up for a moment?" I asked shyly, the red blooming on my cheeks again.

"Of course." He pulled his stone hard body off of mine, adjusting on the seat.

Biting my lip, I said, "Exactly the opposite." Holding my skirts up, I sat on his waiting lap. "I want to feel more of you."

My lips found his as I rocked against him. Knowing we weren't going to go any further emboldened me. I chased that feeling again, wanting nothing more than to cry out against him one more time.

"Who am I to tell a lady no," he murmured in between kisses.

We spent several more minutes moving against each other, chasing pleasure in the small room that twenty-nine other women sat in today.

I knew now that there were only two ways this competition could go. My bargains with the princes could end as the best decisions I've ever made, or the worst ones.

CHAPTER SIXTEEN

Sitting in the dining room, the queen absent as Rowan said, I couldn't help but feel flushed. I barely spoke, neither did Eliza beside me, as we ate in silence. I snuck glances when I felt bold enough to, finding that Dre had a lot easier of a time keeping up normal appearances than I. He acted with Serena as if it was a usual day, not that he was making out with someone who was supposed to be dating his brother a few minutes before.

"Are you alright, Madeline? You seem ill," Reign asked, leaning toward me at the long table.

Jumping up, my face reddened as I looked back at him. "Yes, I'm alright, Your Highness. Thank you. It was a long day in the plaza, I think the heat got the best of me."

"Right, you had to wait the longest of us. That must have been taxing," Curse Breaker Ana said. She dipped her head as if in sympathy, but I felt the dig all the same.

"My brother called on you last?" Reign asked, glancing at the head table where Dre sat.

"Yes," I answered, waiting to see if he'd ask more. I imagined he may try to talk to me about it in private. I cursed, realizing I should have asked Dre if he wanted to keep this from his brother or not. Looking at the way Reign's eyes sought mine and then looked to his brother, he may have already thought it.

Despite the flush, I felt clearer than I had at the ball. Reign was my friend, one I hoped could become my best friend. I wanted what was best for him, and that must have been the reason for my jealousy. He wasn't someone I could have, neither of them were, but Reign and I could be friends for life. After he picked his bride and Thailor returned age to us, I could even visit the palace now and then. He'd be with me forever, while Dre would find someone to be his true queen after Serena, and I wouldn't ever touch him again.

I'd enjoy my and Dre's time together, we certainly had chemistry, but cultivating my friendship with Reign mattered more.

"Thank you for checking on me, Your Highness," I

said with a smile, digging my spoon into the custard in front of me. "I trust you had a good day?"

No, even if Dre said it was fine, I wouldn't tell Reign. At least not yet. We just became friends and I didn't want to jeopardize it with anything. Brothers, especially royal ones, had enough baggage between them.

"I did, thank you. I had meetings with many of the people from the ball yesterday. There is a betting pool among the people, it seems, on who will win."

Eudora's eyebrow raised. "Oh really, who did they think had the most princess material?"

Reign kept his expression neutral, talking about how it was close between a few different people, but no one was significantly in the lead in the eyes of the people. Yet.

Someone else called him into conversation and the murmuring continued. My eyes followed him throughout the meal, studying the chemistry he had with the other contestants. I don't know what was distracting Eliza, but I needed to see who else could be an option if her unease didn't clear. A princess should be confident and clear in her choice. Maybe the people were right, because I didn't think anyone stood out as the front runner yet either. But we had time, there was a month before the eliminations.

Peeking at Dre when I couldn't hold it back anymore, I found his eyes already on mine. I turned away before he did, smiling into my napkin.

"I wonder what they'll have us do next," Eliza said beside me, the first words she spoke to me since we talked briefly at the plaza.

"Yes, I wonder," I murmured, taking another bite.

<hr>

Despite the awkwardness that was growing between me and Eliza, we sat together again the next day in the plaza. They instructed us to wear form-fitting clothes, presumably for a physical activity. Hopefully not running.

"Welcome, Curse Breakers. I am Carley, part of the committee. We have a unique challenge for you today to judge your ability to help the royal family and Prince Reignold."

A group of unfamiliar men and women stood around Carley. I gulped as I observed them, noting they had bows and arrows strapped on their backs and some even had swords.

"As we mentioned, no one is leaving until the end of the first month, so this activity today is only to get a baseline of your ability to protect the prince, physically. As time goes on, we will test for improvements."

Rosamund raised her hand and Carley called on her. Rosamund introduced herself before asking, "Why would we need to learn to fight? Wouldn't a bodyguard do that?"

Voices in the crowd agreed, but it seemed obvious to me. The prince's wife would be his last line of defense if all else failed in an emergency.

"Being royal is a high profile position and that means having contingency plans. There are guards around the princes at all times in public, often hidden and watching while you are unaware. However, anything can happen, and they don't follow the princes within the castle," she explained.

Pacing in front of us, she continued. "Every member of the royal family is trained in combat so they can escape should someone get past the guards or attack them while in private. The risk of a royal family member being hurt in a time where no heir can be created was too great, so we started this training after the Ageless Blight began. The winning Curse Breaker will train until they match the skill of the guards and royal family, even after the curse is lifted."

There were several nods across the plaza as people

grew accustomed to the idea. It wouldn't be pretty, but the logic was there.

"You will be organized in groups, with Serena, Prince Dredrick, and Prince Reignold leading with our esteemed trainers here." She gestured to the intimidating men and women beside her. "We'll test your skills with a bow, a sword, and hand-to-hand combat. Then, based on your initial skills, you'll be assigned a trainer to work with several times a week during your stay at the castle. You'll be tested again toward the end of the month before narrowing to the final five."

While Carley droned on, Eliza leaned to whisper to me.

"This is one thing I don't expect to be good at," she said.

"I've never been one to exercise," I admitted. "But maybe it'll be fun. I hear people say it's great for stress relief."

They called our names, letting us know what trainer to follow, and we lined up. Eliza and I were in separate groups, so we bid each other goodbye and followed our trainers through the garden to an open field a few minutes past it. Waiting in the field were Serena, Reign, and Dre, standing separately from each other in a wide triangle. My trainer led me straight to Reign, and I waved at him with joy. Eliza's group walked to Dre. Eudora, to her horror, was placed with Serena. I'm *sure* they'd be besties.

"Welcome, Curse Breakers," Reign said. "Like Carley explained, we are all going to work in groups to evaluate your primary skills. Once we know how you fare, you'll each be assigned a trainer for the month. If you aren't good at this right away, don't worry. My brother can attest to how bad I was when we first started this training together."

"He was pretty disastrous," Dre called out, projecting from his corner.

My eyes were drawn to Dre and the Curse Breakers he had around him. Something looked off about them. When I focused, looking between those I was with and those with Serena, Dre's group was markedly smaller, with Eliza, Rosamund, and other women I didn't know. He had six people with him, with the Reign and Serena having twelve each.

The teams must have been intentionally chosen, because if they split people evenly his group wouldn't be a few people smaller than the rest. Did Dre pick these people himself, or did he just not have the time to look over as many people as Serena and Reign?

More words of encouragement were said before

weapons were passed out. To start, we were given bows based on our height. Our group trainer, Jake, explained how we were supposed to hold it and how to nock back the arrow. The bow was surprisingly strong and difficult to draw. When it was my turn to hit the target, my arrow fell a foot in front of me, arms shaking from the effort to pull the string back. Thankfully, I wasn't the only one that failed spectacularly, and we all laughed it off.

Next was the sword. They had a few different types. Some were long and broad, made for those that could carry and balance more weight, while others were thinner and lighter, best for cuts and shallow stabs rather than chopping off an arm. When it was my turn and I felt the different sizes, Jake suggested I use a long dagger instead of a sword, pulling one from a sheath on his arm.

"Try this," he said, handing it over.

It weighed less than the sword, but was longer than most of the knives. At his instruction, I gave a few practice thrusts.

"It's like it was made for you," Jake complimented before he moved on to the other girls.

Once every Curse Breaker had a weapon selected, Jake and Reign arranged us in a formation for practice drills. "We aren't going to practice sword fighting in pairs until we get to month two, but you will continue these drills with your trainer in the coming weeks. Some will continue on with archery should they have an affinity for it, but swords and hand-to-hand are required so you can better escape any potential threats."

I listened to his instructions and followed along as Jake and Reign showed us the moves. It was repetitive but oddly relaxing to do the punches and kicks in a rhythm, holding a weapon, and changing sides every ten moves.

When we were good and sweaty an hour later, Jake went around with a clipboard and let everyone know who would be their trainer and the time of their first meeting. I noticed a few people complaining about the activity. They'd never make it to month two with that attitude. To my surprise, Jake said he would be teaching me himself. Our first meeting was set for two days from now.

Reign wished us goodbye when the session was over, eyes lingering on me when I glanced back. I smiled at him, dying to talk.

Like the previous two days, we cleaned up and went to dinner. I was very glad to be out of the athletic outfit. This time, Reign escorted Ana out for a private meal. She was also in the group with Dre—I wonder if he had recommended her to his brother after our interviews with him the night before.

At dinner, as we all stood up to leave, Dre's eyes caught mine and he subtly shook his head no. My heart raced, knowing he meant for me to wait. I took my time, saying I wanted seconds of the dessert, as the other women started to exit the hall, grumbling about how it wasn't fair they hadn't had a turn with the prince yet.

"I'll meet you later, Serena," Dre said, kissing her on the cheek as she walked away.

There were only three people left in the room: me, him, and Lucinda from Wing B.

"How about I walk you ladies out?" Dre said, standing up and making his way over.

"That would be lovely, thank you," Lucinda said. She daintily patted her mouth with a napkin, rising from her chair.

When I stood, the chair scraped behind me noisily and I grimaced. Lucinda giggled behind her hand like I was sideshow entertainment. My face flushed and I looked up at Dre to see him smiling at me sweetly, like I was the cutest thing he had ever seen. My flush deepened.

Walking together, Dre kept cordial conversation going before dropping off Lucinda at her wing. In the distance, Victoria walked out of a room with crumpled linens. Rosamund closed the door behind her, already in her sleep dress.

When we were alone, Dre turned to me in the empty hall with a click of his tongue. "Now, what should I do with you, my favorite little Curse Breaker?"

He stepped forward and I backed up until I hit the wall. His eyes traveled over me, my hands braced on the wallpaper. The seconds that ticked away in silence were heavy. My breath filled the space between us with too loud a hush. His hand trailed up my arm, settling on my shoulder with a light touch.

"You should kiss me," I said, luxuriating in being called his favorite.

His breath mingled with mine, kisses lingering up my neck and to my ear. "You would make a beautiful painting," he whispered. "The way the light hits you, how your brown eyes tell me what you are thinking, how every dress you wear looks like it was sewn just to highlight your hips."

To demonstrate, he gripped them, and I inhaled sharply.

"But I most enjoy the way you moan into my mouth when I grind against you. I've been thinking about it all day, how you squirmed under me last night. You want that now, don't you? You want to moan under me?" Prince Dredrick asked.

Not trusting my voice, I nodded.

His head leaned down, his height considerably taller than mine. Hands moving again, he gripped both of mine, pulling them up with fingers entwined. We were a chain, linked together by our fingers, inseparable but for the lock in my heart. We may as well have been in a dungeon, our hands trapped against the wall, with only our bodies to entertain us.

I met his lips, lifting up my chin. It was gentle, but impassioned.

"I'm hungry for you, dear Madeline, so hungry," he murmured against my lips.

"We should go somewhere more private," I said, glancing around the dim hall. Feet sounded in the distance, far enough that they couldn't see, but that could change any moment. We could get caught.

Dre smiled wickedly, eyes sparkling in a way that made my heart beat faster. "Oh really? You know I said we would not be intimate with each other during this arrangement. Are you asking me to reconsider?" His voice dropped, sending shivers down my spine.

"Shush," I said in a low whisper, "I meant that we are a little exposed here." I glanced again down the hall. We were only feet away from the bedrooms of other Curse Breakers. Anyone could see us if they just peeked outside their door or if staff came back to do some cleaning.

"Hmm..." He released our hands, stepped back, and put his finger to his chin like he was thinking. "There is one place where I could efficiently ravish you, and you can be as loud as you want. Sound can come in, no sound will come out. But, can you keep a secret?"

"I'm very good at secrets," I said quickly, then realized I probably sounded overeager. My cheeks burned at my brazenness. I mean, I *was* overeager, but I didn't want him to know that.

Smiling, he tugged me out of the hall, stopping by a statue that separated Wings A and B.

"Don't tell a soul, little dove," he said, then pushed the tapestry behind the statue to reveal a door.

"*Oh*," I said, surprised. A rush of excitement surged through me.

"It's one of the many royal hiding spots around the palace, for emergencies."

"Is it okay that you are showing it to me?" I asked as he opened the door. I meant it when I said I would keep his secret, but this was something related to his safety. I'm surprised he'd trust me with something like this when we just started to get to know each other.

"Are you going to cause an emergency, little dove?" he teased, his grin infectious.

"No," I said with a smile.

"Then we'll be fine. Just don't tell anyone else, this is for us. Plus, as your *royal tutor*," he said with a wink, referencing our library joke, "this emergency process is helpful to know."

I tumbled into the room after him, hand threaded in his. At first I couldn't see anything, clutching Dre in the dark.

"I've got you, just a moment," he said. There was rustling and then what sounded like the snap of a twig before light filled the room from a lit sconce on the wall.

My eyes adjusted and the room came into view. It was small, about the size of my palace bathroom, but had a few necessities. There was a bed on one end, a chamber pot in the corner, and a shelf with some stored food and dry goods in jars. It had the essentials for a few days, but clearly wasn't meant for a long-term siege if there was one. Tonight, it stood as a secret rendezvous for us.

"It really is a little hideaway," I commented, taking it in.

"If there was some sort of raid on the castle, this would be one of the places the family could hide for a few days. It's quiet, and there is less danger of us being caught here than in your rooms," he said, leading me with him until we sat on the small bed.

The air was thick with anticipation, my breaths shallow as I waited for him to make the first move. Despite his joke, I knew this wouldn't go further than kissing and touching, but I'd be lying if I didn't wish for a repeat of the night before. And more.

His lips were a centimeter from mine when a scream sounded in the distance.

CHAPTER SEVENTEEN

"This was not meant to be a demonstration of the room's safety measures," Dre said and jumped up, hands clenched. "Stay here, little dove, I'll see what's happening."

"No, Dre, don't go." I stepped in front of the door, my hands out. The anticipation I felt moments ago now transformed into a cocktail of fear and adrenaline. "This is a safe place. You are supposed to stay here when there is danger, you *just* told me that. Let me check instead."

He reached for the doorknob and I clutched his shirt. No, there was danger, he had to stay hidden.

In the distance, another scream, sharp and desperate, cut through the small room. I jumped with my own scream.

"I should go instead," I said, but who the hell am I kidding that I could do anything about it?

Dre pulled my chin up, staring me in the eyes. He kissed me for a soft moment. "Madeline, I'm the white knight here. Let me protect you. I'll be fine. I'll see what is happening and be back in ten minutes. Don't come out until I get you and tell you it's safe, okay? Here—" he reached into his pocket and pulled something out, "—take my pocket watch, so you know when to expect me."

Without looking down, I clutched the cold metal, my eyes tearing up.

He pulled a hidden dagger from under his sleeve and gently pushed me away from the door. "I'm locking it from the inside. No one can come in unless you let them in, okay? Wait for me," he instructed. Dre opened it only as much was required for him to sidestep out, so I couldn't see anything beyond the darkness of the tapestry.

Walking backwards, I sat back on the bed and looked down at the watch. It was silver, shining, with etchings on it. I turned it around to see the grooves and found an inscription that read *Endless Ally*.

Was this a gift from Serena or an ex? I puzzled over it, my fingers running over and again atop the carved message.

Turning it back around I watched the seconds tick by, blood rushing in my ears. With each minute that passed, I felt a claw grip tighter on my heart. Why hadn't he come yet? Did Dre get hurt? If he did, would anyone even know I was here? How long should I wait before I venture out on my own?

When twenty minutes passed, I jumped up and paced the small room, shaking out my body and hands to release trapped energy. Tears streamed down my face as my breath hitched. I angrily wiped them every few steps, having no grip on what could be happening outside these walls.

A knock broke my panic and my heart leapt to my throat. Shaking, I walked toward the sound. "Who's there?" I asked, putting my ear to the door.

"Madeline, it's me," a familiar voice said.

"Reign?" I cried out, pulling back the lock and wrenching the door open. "Are you okay? Are we under attack?"

He leaned in from the doorway, holding the tapestry back with one hand, taking in my wide eyes.

"No, we're okay. You can come out. Dre told me he was walking you back from dinner and threw you in here when the scream sounded. I came to get you. He's dealing with the situation."

I put the watch into my dress pocket and stepped out. "Are you sure it's safe?" I asked, feeling guilty that I only thought of Dre the last few minutes and not of my friend.

"Yes, it's okay. If not, I'd jump in there with you," he said, eyes sweeping over my face and then my dress.

The redness of my face and swollen eyes were unmistakable. He pushed a stuck piece of hair back behind my ear.

"Reign, I was so scared," I whispered in the hall, watching as servants ran past us. My eyes followed them, noting their destination had to be Wing B. "What happened?"

"Let me get you to your room and we'll talk along the way," he said, extending his elbow.

I looped my arm through his and took my first deep breath in several minutes. His presence calmed me.

"One of the Curse Breakers took a weapon from training today and turned it on other contestants," he explained in a low whisper.

My eyes shot to his. "Who was it? Was she caught?"

"Yes, Dre caught her. It was Lucinda. She killed Lyra and Kieran. They are being prepared for the Deadlands now, and Lucinda will receive permanent death."

Decapitation. While many people could *live* in

many stages of unending during the blight, if someone's head was cut off or smashed repetitively, it was as close to death as you could be, even though their bodies would not decompose. If your brain can't repair itself, you wouldn't remain conscious.

"Oh god," I said, stopping in the middle of the hall. "I was walking with Lucinda. Dre—I mean, Prince Dredrick was walking us both back from dinner. She could have done that to us."

If Dre hadn't cut off his conversation with her so we could go off and kiss in secret, would we be on the way to the Deadlands too?

Reign faced me, rubbing his hands over my arms soothingly. "You are safe. Nothing is going to happen to you."

"But your brother, he could have died," I said, eyes watering. "We were just with her. Why did she snap like that?"

He paused, taking in my expression, before he said, "Dre can handle himself. You don't need to worry. Focus on yourself, okay? Dre has enough people worrying about him."

I nodded numbly, looking down. Were Lyra and Kieran conscious enough of what was happening? Was it painful? I hoped Dre was able to comfort them before they left for the Deadlands.

Thirty Curse Breakers, now twenty-seven.

"Hey," Reign said softly, calling my attention back to him.

I looked up, tears falling.

"This was an exhausting day, our first day of training, and then this scenario?" He shook his head, rubbing his hands up and down my arms soothingly. "It's horrible that these women lost their lives. You need to rest. I'm cancelling everything tomorrow while we deal with this and I check on everyone. Go lie down, sleep in, and I'll check on you tomorrow, okay?"

With a watery smile, I agreed, and he pulled me into a hug. Reign ran his hands over my hair until I calmed down. Melting into his embrace, I took in deep inhales of his honey scent. I could spend all day in his arms and still feel welcomed, like Reign was a blanket and a book waiting for me in bed on a rainy day.

After a few minutes, I pulled back and looked him in the eyes. "Thank you," I whispered.

"I'll always be here for you, Madeline," he said softly, fingers rubbing the base of my neck.

It was as if time had slowed down as we looked at each other in the dark of the hall, neither of us moving.

Dre was fire and ice at the same time, the elements of destruction and rebirth. It was exhilarating every time we were together.

But Reign? He was like water, calm and serene, but under the right circumstances, just as devastating.

I didn't know how to reconcile it.

Before my brain could come to any conclusions, someone called for Reign from the end of the hall and the moment shattered. He answered them and took my hand, walking me the last few feet to my door.

"Stay inside, alright?" His eyes searched mine in the dark, seeming to hesitate.

"Be safe, Reign," I replied.

With a sad smile I closed the door, leaning my forehead against its cold surface.

That night, I laid under the covers, clutching Dre's watch as I read the inscription again and again. He had said he would be back, but sent his brother. Logically, he wouldn't be coming, but I couldn't get my eyes to close. If I knew how to get to him, I would have checked on him, and he knew where I was, so wouldn't he come check on me?

Idiot, I scolded myself. This is a prince I kissed twice. He's not my boyfriend and doesn't owe me a check-in. Just because I was a bleeding heart that would have checked on him, doesn't mean he owes me the same courtesy.

My eyes lifted to the door, and I squinted as if that would help me hear better. Did I imagine it... a muffled sob? It may just be my imagination, or the stress from the day, but just in case...

Getting up, I tiptoed to the door and reached for the handle. My heart was thrumming a nervous rhythm in my chest, and I pushed it down, opening the door a crack.

No, not imagined. Someone was crying, the sound clearer now, with little gasps escaping like they couldn't breathe.

Pushing the wood farther, I peeked out. The hallway was dimly lit, but I could make out two figures in the hall. Eudora was there, a vision in a long silk nightgown, her face streaked with tears.

Prince Reignold was in front of her, consoling her, his posture a picture of concern. They spoke in soft whispers, too far away for me to hear.

My stomach churned. This was a private moment, I shouldn't look. As I started to pull back the door, Reign dipped his head and their lips met softly.

I froze, hand still on the knob. My brain felt like it was short-circuited, unable to understand what was happening as my world tilted on an axis. Was this their first kiss, here in the dark outside her room?

Closing the door, I leaned against it, sliding down. It didn't matter that he liked Eudora, I told myself. Sure, bad choice, but it was his to make. I'm just his friend, the friend that was kissing his brother in the dark. He could make whatever mistake he wanted to.

This was his journey to love, not mine.

Not mine.

Eventually I drifted off into a troubled slumber, with no one by my side.

CHAPTER EIGHTEEN

The next morning, Victoria came by to let me know that there were now ten fewer contestants. Other than the three involved in the incident, seven others asked to go home after talking with Reign. Thirty became twenty in the blink of an eye.

I stayed in bed, reading the prophecy again. There had to be something else I could do to break this curse and keep the princes, and myself, safe. Even if one of them was off kissing my enemy.

Clutching Dre's watch, I pored over the prophecy and my notes, my thumb running over the cool metal edge again and again like it could conjure answers.

My eyes caught, reading the same line again and again. Wait—

> *While some may heal,*
> *the rest will fester*
> *with allies in their tomb.*

I looked down at the watch. *Endless Ally*, the inscription said. *Ally* to the prince. Who gave this to him? Were they an ally to his tomb? Was he going to die?

A chill broke over my skin. I sketched the watch beside the passage. What other clues did I miss?

Quick knocks sounded at the door. Dre?

I stood up, straightening my wrinkly shirt and pants and running my hand through my knotty hair. I paused with a hand on the knob. Two women were murdered for opening their door just the night before.

"Who is it?" I asked, voice cracking from disuse.

"Eliza," her small voice replied.

I threw open the door in relief. "Hi, come in."

Eliza walked through the opening, her tangy floral perfume wafting through the air as she moved to sit on my bed. She wore the full black training outfit we were all given. However, hers was long-sleeved and a turtle-neck collar, like she always wore.

"Are you okay?" I asked, noticing her pinched expression.

"I am going to take Prince Reignold's offer and go

home," Eliza said, glancing at me before looking around the room. Her gaze snagged on my notes for a moment, before moving on.

"Because of the attacks?" I asked. Was she worried more people would get hurt? No one was supposed to leave until the month was over, yet one third of the Curse Breakers were already gone, one way or another. Lucinda was captured, surely this wouldn't happen again.

"Yes and no. What happened was shocking, of course, but it only highlighted that I was wasting time being here," she explained.

"It's only been a week, hardly time wasted," I reasoned. "You've only been on one date with him. Who knows what could happen after the next one?"

Please don't go.

"That's the problem. I don't have time to grow to like him," she said.

"I know the committee said Prince Reignold would narrow down the Curse Breakers after a month, but the timetable is out the window now isn't it? Nothing has gone to plan, so if the prince needs more time, I'm sure they'll give it to him." I tried to explain. One date doesn't determine their entire future.

Eliza shook her head, hesitating as she opened and closed her mouth before saying, "Madeline, I'd like to trust you with something. It's a risk for me to share, but I need you to understand, and protect yourself."

"Of course you can trust me. We're friends," I said. "Are you okay?"

Eliza looked down, wringing her hands. "This is hard to say."

I knelt on the floor in front of her, taking her hands. They were cold, so I rubbed my hands over hers to calm her nerves. "Whatever it is, I'm here for you."

Her eyes watered. "I'd rather spend the time I have left, at home, with my family."

"What do you mean?" I asked, holding my breath.

"I'm Unending," she said, and time seemed to slow.

Eliza released my hand, reaching up to pull down her collar, showing a red gash. Her throat was slit low on her neck and dry coagulated blood rimmed the opening. It was dried in layers, nearly black.

I gasped, eyes wide in horror. I almost reached forward to cover the mark, as if I could stop what had already happened, but I held back. "Did Lucinda get you in the attack and you hid it? Does it hurt? Are you okay?" The words tumbled out of me before I could stop them, shocked and confused. I cursed at myself, *of course* she wasn't okay and *of course* it hurt.

"No, it wasn't Lucinda. I've been dead for years,"

Eliza explained, her tone calm and resigned, used to her life, despite the gravity of her words.

"When I came here, forced as one of the Curse Breakers, I knew it would mean I wouldn't survive to see the curse lifted. Now that the prince has given us an out, I'm going to take it and go home. I thought about staying to help you win, but I need to be home."

"Eliza, I'm so sorry," I said, choking down a sob. I dropped my head to the hand she still held in mine. My breath came in gasps, and each one was a stab to my beating heart.

Doing the right thing, ending this curse, would permanently kill her. Gone.

Conceptually, I knew many people would no longer walk Riversend after this, but the Unending seemed so far removed from my life when I could see children like Flora suffering.

I was close to so few people that I hadn't had to experience it—the slow grief of someone I cared about dying, walking among the world. With my parents, death came and took them, then the Ageless Blight came after.

The only people I had in my life were Flora and Hester.

Flora, unable to solve that puzzle, hitting it again and again each morning, not able to grow up.

Saving Flora would doom Eliza.

Thailor was cruel to allow this pain. I rarely thought of the gods, except for an occasional phrase or even joke, but they were at the core of this.

"Don't be sorry, Madeline. I've had more years of life than I ever would have because of the blight." Despite her assurances, she stumbled on the words. "I'm lucky. And now, you will bring back life and progress to those I leave behind. I'm ready to die, I just want to do so surrounded by family."

She sat on the floor beside me, holding on to me tightly. When I pulled away and took a deep breath, the tangy scent was more apparent. It was blood. This whole time, her perfume was covering the smell of her blood.

Eliza, I'm so sorry.

Realizing what she was going through in secret only made me sob harder. "Who did this to you?" I could barely make out the words.

"Madeline, please, I have more to tell you, but you need to remain calm," she explained. "This isn't about me or my murderer, I took care of that already. Listen closely to what I have to say, okay?" She wiped my tears and rubbed my back.

I nodded, trying to gather myself back together for her.

"Being an Unended is not like people say it is. There are many of us that can continue to live mostly normal lives, like myself, avoiding the Deadlands," Eliza explained. "Many of them don't want the blight to end, so they can keep on with their lives."

She sighed, tucking a hair behind her ear. "I can understand why they feel like that, but as you know, there are more vulnerable people out there than the dead, and we have to think of them. But—"

Eliza paused, looking at my face.

I whispered, "What is it?"

"You have to be careful, Madeline," Eliza said, gripping my hand tighter. "I am not the only Unending in the castle..."

CHAPTER NINETEEN

"You aren't?" I asked. Sweat prickled my skin, my beating heart racing like it might escape my chest.

"No, we can recognize others like ourselves. This castle is full of the dead, but I won't name them. I wouldn't want to jeopardize what time anyone has left, but it's more common than you'd think. The only dead that go to the Deadlands are those that died in public or those that were too far gone to hide. The dead surround you and they won't go quietly," Eliza said, voice dire. "We go to great lengths to hide ourselves."

She held up her hands, pushing back the sleeve to show her burns. They stopped before her elbow. "I burned my hands on purpose, to give an excuse for why I'd need to cover my neck. It makes hiding easier, to pretend I survived a fire. Burns by itself aren't a death sentence, so it gave me a plausible lie. Not everyone can fake it but many do."

My eyes widened, horrified by the decisions the Unending had to make to keep safe. And I knew more of the dead? My brain imagined all the people around me, the twenty-nine women... well, less now. But Mitchell, the party planners, the attendants and staff of the castle, the royal family, so many new people that I've surrounded myself with. Under the royal family's noses, the dead *live* and work here? Who? How many?

A thought occurred to me. "Was Lucinda already Unending, before she was given permanent death? Was she dead the whole time?"

"No." Eliza shook her head. "She was not dead before the attack, but it's possible this wasn't her idea. I can't think of any reason for her to kill Lyra and Kieran so messily. If she was trying to get rid of the competition, she would have been more subtle and would have started with you or me since we are the closest to the prince so far."

The thought was sobering. Eliza was right. Lucinda had been too easy to catch. She was either very bad at murder—which was a good thing to be awful at, in my opinion—or this wasn't her idea.

"Some of the Unending can persuade the living to

do our bidding," Eliza continued. "It's a rare power, more common in those that already had their souls taken by Veyra, becoming their mirror selves. Their voices can carry the power of suggestion over the living. If they tell you to do something, it'll seem like it's your idea."

A wave of horror washed over me. "Thank you for trusting me," I said slowly, brow furrowed as panic struck me in waves. "I'll try and be careful, but I'm not sure what precautions I could take. How can I stop myself from being a victim to something like this?" I worried my lip, feeling hopelessness sink into my stomach at the thought that someone could have that kind of power over me.

"I actually have something to help with that," Eliza said, reaching into her pocket.

Eliza handed me a thin silver necklace with two small silver balls attached on separate clasps. It had a long chain, easy to tuck into my dresses. I held it up to the light, noticing the balls felt heavy, with a seam along the middle of them as if they could open. I thumbed it and Eliza shook her head. "Don't open them."

"What do they do?" I asked.

"It's my blood. You'll still seem alive to other Unending, it won't fool them, but it will keep their influence from penetrating you. Wear it, but hide it if you can," she warned.

"Why do I need to hide it?" I asked, putting it around my neck. I didn't feel any different, but if Eliza said it would protect me, I had to try.

"If an Unending saw you with it, they'd know you were close with another person like them, and that can be threatening. These are usually given to family members we want to protect, like spouses or children. Our secrets must be kept, or we are in danger of being forced into a permanent death. I've given you two, just in case you need to give one to the prince for protection as well."

Looking down at the thin silver chain, I took a deep breath. This was a lot to take in. "Thank you, Eliza, for protecting me and for giving me a spare. We haven't known each other long, but I care about you. I'm so sorry for what has happened to you. I'm sorry for trying to push you to date Reign, that must have been upsetting."

"No, you have been a great friend to me. You were only trying to do what you thought was right. I've had enough time, more than anyone should. I'm ready to die for good. I just want to be with my family when you complete the prophecy."

"But it's not me," I said, denying it. "I don't want to marry the prince."

Eliza shook her head, lips tight. "Madeline..." she

started, "it has to be you, and now another qualification fits you."

"What do you mean?" I whispered.

"*The Summer Maiden learns the truth of the dead*," she recited. "It's not just about who we lost before, but what we know now. You know the truth of the dead, I just told you."

I gasped, pulling away from my friend and pacing the room. Anger stormed me, like she forced my hand and made me the prophecy's maiden without considering my own choices. Pausing, I took a deep breath. In and out, I gave myself a moment to process.

I'd have wanted to know what was happening with Eliza regardless of a prophecy. And didn't I try to force Eliza to be the Summer Maiden by encouraging the prince to date her?

It would be hypocritical of me to blame her for helping me along with the prophecy when I was encouraging the prince to choose her in the same way.

Turning back to her, I said, "But I don't love the prince, not in that way."

"You've studied the prophecy as much as I have. You know that your love is not needed," she said slowly but not unkindly.

Nodding, I studied the floor, closing the subject in

my mind. This conversation should not be about me, not when I was going to lose Eliza forever.

"I don't want you to die," I whispered, a tear falling down my cheek as I clutched the necklace she gave me.

Eliza pulled me into a hug again, stroking my back soothingly as she whispered, "I've had a good life. It will be okay."

No, it wasn't okay, but it was right. For Flora, for the children, for those that loved the vulnerable—like Hester —and felt helpless to save them, and even for the Unending. For those in forever pain, they had time to make their choices, to live past what life would have given them. It was time to say goodbye and start the world again.

We talked for another hour, Eliza giving me insight into what being an Unending was like for her, before she said it was time for her to go.

"Be wary of who you trust, Madeline," she said at the door. "The dead close in. Not only on you, but on Prince Reignold. Train, okay? Stay by his side."

"I'll be careful. Thank you, Eliza," I said, my heart cracking in my chest. My first friend in decades, slipping from my fingers, who would die the moment I fulfilled the prophecy.

As much as I tried to tell myself this wasn't about me, I couldn't pretend any longer.

"Goodbye, Madeline. I'm rooting for you," Eliza said, closing the door behind her.

"Goodbye," I whispered into the empty room, knowing somehow that this was only the beginning.

The kingdom was unraveling around me. The lies that kept it moving, the Unending walking among us, slowly souring as their soul sought the goddess of death —it all led me to the same conclusion.

The wheel halts a millennia for respite; those that would have died continued, healing or not, a reprieve they received from death.

With allies in their tomb, the unfolding trickles blood in the tapestry of wounds; the dead have help, integrating into our broken society.

Together, they hold two souls, two paths—a curse lifted or restored. Woven in dread her heart must be forged; Reign and I have work to do, no matter the pain or what happens next.

Entwined in stolen grief their crowned paths may be, for all and for each other, for one loves the other in a tale of sight and gold; I tried to ignore the looks Reign gave me, but I knew.

A petal fell onto my vanity, the rose from Prince Reignold wilting.

With the second-born prince, enthralled and newly wed.

"Good form," Prince Reignold said, coming up from behind me.

I turned my head, managing a breathless greeting, in between hitting Jake's gloved hands. The sweat stung my eyes and dripped down my back, leaving a cold trail in its wake.

"Would you like to sub in, Your Highness?" Jake asked, already pulling off his gloves.

Reign nodded, taking Jake's spot in front of me and putting on the protective gloves. He wore a sleeveless shirt and a sheen of sweat along the top of his chest, having just finished his own session.

Eliza's words had repeated in my head over the week since she left. *The dead close in. Train. I've been* working with Jake every day since, even though I was only required to meet with him twice a week.

Jake took it in stride, glad I was committed to learning more.

Did Reign know there were Unending in his castle? Did Jake? Having this information made me question everything.

I've hardly seen anyone except Jake and Victoria following the incident. Group meals were suspended as they did security sweeps, food was brought to our rooms instead. Sometimes I'd see another contestant walking down the hall, or heard whispers from closed rooms while on my way to my fighting practice, but not enough to know more of what was happening. Reign checked on me every other day, but they were only quick conversations. I hadn't seen Dre at all, not since he ran off to be a hero.

"We're practicing formation three," Jake said.

"It's okay, you just got back from your session. I don't want to inconvenience you," I said, wiping the sweat from my forehead. It was exhausting, but the burn was welcome at the same time. When so much was out of control, these workouts helped me feel like I had that power back.

"Worried you'll hurt me, Madeline?" Reign asked with a smirk, lifting his hands as if in surrender.

Rolling my eyes good-naturedly, I followed my moves but pulled my punches until I felt more assured. Reign drilled me through the left, right, left jabs, encouraging me to move faster and harder. By the tenth rotation, I was no longer holding back, pushing my limbs harder than I had all week.

Reign was laughing, following through on each move with me. "Faster," he said. "You've got it."

I followed his instructions, feeling the burn in my shoulders. Sweaty strands fell from my braid, smacking my face with each jab.

His voice sounded rougher when he said, "Make me hurt, Madeline. Hit me harder."

The command rasped through the air, low and hungry, sparking something in me. As we danced faster around the ring, he egged me on. His grin wasn't of someone winning but of someone proud.

By the time Jake blew his whistle signaling for us to stop our drills, Reign and I had gone through five different types of moves and combinations, *formations* as Jake called them, and my heart was hammering.

"Good job, Madeline, you'll be my star pupil soon enough. You better watch out, Your Highness," Jake joked.

"I bet you say that to everyone you train," I said and plopped to the ground inelegantly. If I weren't so tired, I probably would have sucked it up until he left the room, but I didn't have the energy to look cute.

"Actually, I don't." Jake didn't elaborate as he picked up his water bottle and bowed to Reign. "See you tomorrow, Madeline," he called as he walked out the training center.

I waved weakly from my spot on the exercise mat, staring up at the ceiling. Reign looked down at me, his head blocking the window in the ceiling. The glow of a halo seemed to appear around his head.

"Need a minute?" he asked. Despite moving across the mat with me, taking my hits, he was as relaxed as he was when he walked through the door. Just a light film of sweat coated his chest and arms.

I glared at him, not dignifying him with a response. I'd have to learn to control my breathing, maybe I could add some sort of meditation practice.

Reign laid down beside me, our arms lightly grazing each other.

Impulsively, I turned to my side, dropping a hand to his chest. He angled so he could look back, his eyes roaming my face.

"Is everything settled now? Are you ready to get back to finding your wife?" I asked.

When will we be getting married? I thought to myself. It wouldn't be a bad thing, I reasoned. Being alone this week, I'd thought a lot about what Eliza said and my role in the prophecy. If I was the one that could save the living, wouldn't it be worth getting over my fears of being in a public position?

I opened my mouth to tell him, to say I believed that I was the Summer Maiden and for him to actually consider me, but he spoke first.

"I never stopped looking for a wife. I just needed some time to do so privately, in between the security arrangements. These supposed tests from the committee —" He paused, turning from my eyes to look at the ceiling skylight. "—I wanted to explore things without their influence, with *no one's* influence, really. After everything that happened with Lucinda, I needed to make sure everyone here was someone I could see a future with. It's not fair to endanger anyone otherwise."

"Oh, I see," I said, the frog in my throat growing bigger.

He pushed a strand of hair behind my ears. "I've been thinking about the prophecy. There is a particular line, *'for one loves the other.'* It can only mean two things."

"What do you think?" I asked, knowing he'd bring himself to the same conclusion I did, but needing to hear it aloud.

"Either the Summer Maiden loves me and I don't, or

I love the Summer Maiden and she doesn't love me." He turned back to me. "Many of the Curse Breakers could love me for my station in life. As a prince, that is unfortunately the easy part. But being a prince isn't all it's cracked up to be."

Reign's voice cracked, and I felt the sorrow in it. The loneliness that came with his position of power and the difficult choices he had to make.

Holding his hand, I tugged him closer until we were enveloped in a sweaty hug on the floor. He inhaled deeply, his forehead falling down to my shoulder. "I'm your friend, remember?" I whispered, validating his theory without saying it aloud. "You're safe with me, Reign, I promise. Talk to me."

He shook his head against mine, holding me in the silence. His arms shook, as if holding back his pain. I held him back just as tightly, running soothing circles wherever my hands could reach.

After a few minutes, he spoke again. "There are only two people I would consider being with even if I didn't love them, and then two I can see myself loving. One of them is you, as I'm sure you've guessed. And you don't want this."

I inhaled sharply.

While last week I would have said he was right and I didn't want this, there were inklings of change, acceptance, and kinship that had grown since we met. Somehow, someway, being a princess felt like a possibility I'd be willing to do for him, and for even more than that. For Flora, for Eliza, for the vulnerable.

"I've grown to change my opinion on this. Maybe. Just a little," I said in a whisper, scared to admit it out loud.

He pulled back quickly, hands coming to cradle my face.

"You'd consider marrying me?" Reign's eyes swam over mine, a hope alight in them I had yet to see.

"Yes," I said, mouth dry. "I've come to believe I'm the Summer Maiden. But more than that, I think we would be good partners."

He nodded slowly. "What changed your mind?"

Reaching between us, I pulled the necklace Eliza gave me out from under my shirt.

His eyes widened as he held the small spheres, two lockets of blood knocking against each other, before gently tucking them back in my shirt where they couldn't be seen. "The truth of the dead. How long have you known?"

"Yes, a short time," I whispered. "Do you have one to protect yourself?"

He nodded, thoughtful. "Yes, but they are hard to come by."

Biting my lip, I said, "I can't betray who gave them to me."

"I understand. And two, one for me I presume?"

I made a split second decision. "Yes, but if you have one already, give it to the second person you care about. If you don't have extra, I mean."

He searched my face, brushing back my sweaty hair. "Why would you suggest that?"

"I'm your friend, Reign. If you have two potential options, each with the truth of the dead, then you'll be more likely to be okay after this. That's what I want more than anything, for you and our people to be okay."

"Our people..." he echoed, gaze wide with astonishment as he took me in. He was happy that I would say it, even more than I would feel it.

The tears fell freely now. Overcome, I couldn't stop them. "I'm sorry," I whispered, broken and whole at the same time.

"You have nothing to be sorry for, Madeline," he said, tugging me so he could place his head over mine.

There was so much I felt sorry for, even though I knew it wasn't my fault. It was logical for me to have been hesitant about this. To go from a nobody to a princess wasn't something to take lightly, but I felt horrible that he had felt alone in this.

Mourning my old life, the simple one I knew I was

hiding in, and the fairytale of Prince Dredrick that I distracted myself with, I cried. Deeply, unabashedly, I let the tears come and took solace in Reign.

He said he could love me, and I believed him. More than anything else I've been told these weeks, I trusted him.

Surrounded by him, I felt safe enough to be vulnerable. With Reign, it's always been that way, and if I got to be married to a friend that would treat me well and save everyone at the same time... it wouldn't be a bad life.

He kissed my forehead and wiped my tears before helping me stand and taking me in his arms again.

"I've got you, baby. I'll take care of you."

Not a bad life at all.

CHAPTER TWENTY-ONE

Curse Breaker Hall Wing A was as silent as the stars. No sounds of women getting ready behind closed doors, fewer palace servants, and the weight of what had already happened.

Eliminations, without Reign telling me until they had already happened. Was everyone else left in the dark, or just me?

In the middle of the hall, I waited a few minutes before we were scheduled to leave. Who would come out of their room as one of the four Reign thought he could have a future with? Would anyone come out, or were they in Hall B?

It felt like a competition now. This must have been what the other Curse Breakers felt in the beginning, this yearning mixed with hope.

Before, I didn't want it. A lot had changed since that first day. Whomever he picked, whether or not it was me, would help end the Ageless Blight, moving on to get the vital information of their next step from the royal prophet.

What mattered is whom we will save. Those stuck in limbo. People having to watch as their loved ones suffered year after year, living *through* their death, never to rest.

It was time for it all to end. In the new world there would be immense grief, and yet, startling hope.

A door clicked and I turned, loosing a breath when I saw which room it belonged to. The one I least wanted but suspected would be true.

In red, as bright and bold as the day I met her weeks ago, *Eudora*.

Their kiss came to mind, the one I shouldn't have seen. Eudora's tears, fear, and the way he held her face. It was obvious it hadn't been their first one.

He had wiped my tears the day before, kissing my forehead, because I was the one keeping him at arms length.

She slithered up to me, moving in a way that I didn't know how to do, with a wide smile on her face like she knew she had already won.

"Hello, Madeline," she said musically, obviously very pleased with herself.

"Eudora," I greeted carefully, holding my posture tight.

She lifted her hand to push her hair back behind her ears. Her bracelet jingled, a new charm bracelet I hadn't seen her wear before. On it were multiple charms, one being the small silver sphere I had the twin to.

Well, the prince didn't waste any time. She had the gift of protection, originally from Eliza, within the night. And he was less concerned about the items being seen, or at least hoped the other charms would distract from the blood bearing one.

Not one to be shown up, I fingered the chain around my neck, pulling it from under the pink fabric of my dress with a smile.

Her smile dropped, just as I hoped.

"Ah," she hummed. "So you know too." Her lips thinned in displeasure.

"You are right, Eudora, I too know *how horrible this world is*," I hissed, "and am taking it seriously rather than pretending getting a trinket from the prince means that I'm going to walk down the aisle." I felt petty, and truly I was *being* petty, but I hated to see her gloat when this was a serious matter. She didn't have to know the prince didn't give it to me.

But she needed to be less of a bitch, and you fight bitch with bitch.

"Ouch," Eudora said. "Kitten's got claws." She rolled her eyes. "Of course, I know this doesn't mean I've won. But it means anyone other than us likely hasn't. Take the win, kitten. Who knows when you'll get one again?"

Eudora's smile returned and she sashayed past me. I stared after her, knowing she was right.

After a minute in the quiet hall, I followed, placing the necklace back into my dress. It created almost a highlight on my small bust, the silver chain sitting between the swell of my breasts. Thankfully, my dress wasn't a full corset, so I wasn't gasping for breath, but it was more fitted than some of my other outfits. I felt more like an elevated version of myself today, hair down and free-flowing. I didn't put on much makeup, after all the crying yesterday I couldn't bring myself to.

It would be me or Eudora at the end of this, no other option made sense now.

"Hi, Mitchell," I said, finding him talking not far away from the Curse Breaker halls.

"Madeline, I haven't seen you all week."

"I don't think most people saw anyone this week," I commented with a shrug.

"True." He dipped his head in agreement.

"Any clues you can share on what I'm walking into today?"

He considered for a moment, before saying, "I have a feeling it's going to be something you like but also hate at the same time."

Raising my brows, I challenged, "That's not a helpful clue."

"No, it's not," he said with a laugh, walking away. He was an odd one, but I liked that about him.

Rolling my eyes, I pushed open the doors to the plaza.

What greeted me was sobering. In place of the long rows split by a center aisle were four chairs near the dais. Small. Isolating. We were all that was left.

One chair each for myself, Eudora, Amelia, and Rosamund. They all sat waiting, looking at me with various emotions, none positive.

Amelia was nice enough in the brief interactions we'd had. I could see how she could make a good princess. Refined, cute, likely to listen to authority. She was someone I would have expected to win, before I got invested in the results myself. She was similar to Eliza as a quiet forerunner, but more boring. There were worse things someone could be. In truth, I had barely paid attention to the dark skinned and sleek-haired woman.

But Rosamund? While Amelia may respect authority, Rosamund thrived in putting others down for the fun of it, even more so than Eudora. *Vindictive.* I didn't know why Reign would pick her. If he believed he had a potential future with her, what did that mean in relation to me? Eudora was a leader in her own way, though a mean one on occasion. She was a better choice than Rosamund.

Glancing Eudora's way, I eyed her steely expression. She was focused, I'd give her that. That's a good thing in most circumstances.

Rowan walked forward, a somber expression on his face. His sash appeared crumpled, and his eyes were sunken. He did not take this week of change and death well, it seemed.

Clearing his throat, he said, "Hello, Curse Breakers. After the tragic permanent deaths of Lyra and Kieran, we took a break to reevaluate the planned events in the competition, removing some of the more unnecessary elements and focusing on what we could do to help you all and the prince get to know each other, as well as prove yourself to the people. While we live in dangerous times, we don't need to add to the danger here at home."

If only they thought of that before Lucinda was given a dagger from our training ring competition and walked away with it.

After a pause, he continued, "And after further

discussion with Prince Reignold, we made the wise decision to eliminate the contestants to the final four, instead of the initial planned five after the first month. You are those most likely to suit the prophecy and a long-term successful marriage. The committee and the prince believe in you."

It didn't sit well with me how they took credit for the prince's decision. Rowan and the other committee members clapped, as if they actually did something.

"Today's task is meant to build community between our prospective princesses, the royal family, and your fellow citizens. Yes, I know we said the queen would not be involved until later, but with only four Curse Breakers left, now is the time." He gestured to the door that led back into the palace.

Our eyes followed him, finding Reign and behind him, the queen.

Reign walked forward, clapping a hand on Rowan's shoulder, taking over the explanation from there. "We are going to visit the people, our royal orphanage in particular, to remind ourselves who we are doing this for."

Smiling at him, my heart swelled. That was a touching idea. Many of the children didn't understand their lives had been at a standstill, and those that were old enough to understand had often found unhealthy ways to cope.

"We'll leave in ten minutes," he said, voice firm, "all of us." When he looked away from his potential princesses, I followed his line of sight. There stood Dre and Serena, dressed in finery befitting the next king and queen.

I hadn't seen him in days. The absence had felt personal, and I wanted to know why. Why hadn't he visited me after such a frightful night?

As if my thoughts summoned him, Dre's eyes met mine and a mischievous smirk lit up his face. While holding my gaze, my heart racing, he intertwined his fingers with Serena's. She beamed at him, her smile radiant as if she believed the sun was shining from his eyes.

Were Serena's feelings real, or an act like Dre's? For her sake, I hoped they were fake.

Dre's gaze stayed on me a few seconds more before turning to follow Reign out the doors.

I needed to see him. In the week he had left me in silence, so much had changed. And it would be wrong to let it all go unsaid now.

Regardless of how serious or not serious we were, Prince Dredrick Komari wasn't mine, and I wasn't his.

The palace was silent as we walked out the doors. I held up my dress, feeling the weight of it and wishing I had known I'd be meeting more people today before leaving my room. I regretted the little makeup I had chosen. Being *just me* had been fine when it was just for Reign, but that didn't feel good enough for a public outing.

What would the citizens of Riversend think of Reign's decision to narrow the thirty to four so quickly?

The first day here, I had wanted to leave as quickly as possible, helping if I could, but mostly focusing on my escape back to unimportance.

And now here I was, in a secret physical relationship with the heir to the throne that I needed to call off, and hoping to marry his brother.

The queen entered the first carriage of the three on the drive, followed by Dre and Serena.

Rosamund and Amelia entered our carriage first, then Reign helped Eudora into the carriage behind them, gripping her hand to help her get up the step. My heart clenched seeing how nice they looked together, her dark hair beside his golden. They were like two sides of a coin in their beauty but with a matching confidence that I lacked.

I came here as no one. Who was I now?

"Madeline?" Reign asked, extending his hand to me. His soft brown eyes held mine.

Inhaling slowly to calm my nerves, I took his extended hand, but did not step into the carriage yet.

The dimple on his left side visible, he asked, "Are you alright?"

"I will be, I think," I said with a smile, squeezing his hand and entering the carriage.

He came in a second later, sitting across from me on the carriage benches.

Our eyes held, a softness unspoken between us, before he looked away.

CHAPTER TWENTY-TWO

It was difficult to concentrate on the conversation flitting about the carriage. Sitting closest to the door, I leaned against it, eyes closing.

I'd met plenty of children over our long lifetime but had never been to an orphanage. Everbrook was a small enough town that we sent our orphans away to the neighboring larger city. Out of sight, out of mind, but *not really*. The laughter of youth had drained from my hometown, until there was so little of it left that the absence was deafening.

Hopefully soon, we'll be able to give everyone a second chance at life again, *somehow*. Now at the final four, we'd meet the prophet soon, like Rowan told us that first day. We'd get more information then.

Flora can grow up soon, moving past the little

puzzle box she was frustrated over daily. Hester could take her to school in a few years, and if Eudora wins this instead of me, I could help pick up Flora some days. It was a nice idea, helping Hester with her. I hoped she was okay. Maybe I could ask Reign to get a letter to her for me.

"We're about to arrive, Your Highness," a voice said through the curtained window behind me.

Blinking my eyes open, I sat up, posture straightening. The carriage slowed, and the sounds around us increased, cheers and whistles of happy gatherers. I smoothed my dress and wiped my sweaty palms on the seat.

"Just a moment, ladies," Reign said when the carriage came to a stop. "Before we go inside, I wanted to prepare you for something."

"What is it, Prince Reignold?" Amelia asked.

I could barely hear her soft voice over the sounds of the crowd.

"I know there are children in every village, but with the increases in the Unending these last decades, many have come here when the local homes run out of room. There are hundreds in the royal orphanage, with dozens of volunteers to help them. But it's a heartbreak every day." He paused, looking at the closed door in thought. "These children will never truly live if we don't help them. *They* are why I agreed to this competition. They deserve, more than anyone else, for the blight to end. The volunteers you'll meet today are on the front line of a lot of charged emotions. Treat them as well as you'd treat me."

His eyes filled with unshed tears, and I yearned to hold him, to console the broken part of him that was also broken in me.

"We won't let you down," Eudora said, touching a hand to her chest. Her voice took on a seriousness that I didn't expect of her.

Damn it, Eudora, you better not make me change my mind about you.

When Reign nodded at me, I swallowed my feelings and opened the carriage door.

Dre was waiting, his hand palm up for mine. There was a twinkle in his eye, like he had thought something terribly delightful about me.

"Thank you, Your Highness," I said with a smile.

He squeezed my fingers for a second too long before I moved on, making my way to Rowan by the doors of the large building.

We really needed to talk. I had told him I wouldn't marry his brother when this first started, but now it was my goal. Even if things weren't romantic with Reign, at least not yet, I couldn't in good faith continue with his brother.

That wasn't who I wanted to be with my future husband. We were going to be partners, I hoped, and I couldn't start our relationship that way.

A sea of people lined the street, pressed behind barricades and guards calling order. They grew louder at the sight of us, knowing one of the women here would be elevated to princess. How had they felt about going down to four so quickly, I wondered. Was it exciting to know it was almost over, or upsetting to not have more time to chew on the contestants before spitting them back out?

The queen stood in her splendor, stoic as they called her name. The orphanage behind them set an imposing figure with its dark wood, long windows, and multiple stories. There stood a tall domed section toward the back that looked like it could have been a conservatory, where panels would open for stargazing.

"Forever may she reign!" a voice yelled from the crowd.

I turned toward the sound but didn't catch who said it. Did they actually want forever?

The queen blinked, head moving slightly as if she also looked, before turning to enter the building with Dre and Serena following behind.

Reign walked to the crowd, shaking hands and talking, while we stood beside Rowan. I couldn't remember the last time Reign was in the public eye before the competition, as the royal family had stayed away from the people for decades for their safety. Was it typical for him to seem like the one who cared the most?

I stepped forward, ignoring Rowan's protest, and went to the barricades to stand beside him. "Hi, I'm Madeline," I said to the crowd, following Reign as he spoke. He gave me a grateful smile, which I met in kind before taking a gift handed to me. A teddy bear.

"For the children. Thank you for taking the time to see them," the woman said.

"Thank you for bringing a gift for them," I replied. "I know someone in there really needs this bear."

The bear was soft and worn, worn in a way that told me it had already comforted someone through many dark nights. I clutched it to my chest for a moment, grounding myself in the simple kindness of it.

Eudora's laugh broke my concentration. A few feet down, she was also speaking to the crowd. Amelia and Rosamund as well, but they decidedly looked more awkward at it, not touching anyone and standing farther away from the barricade.

Maybe they were smarter. It was safer that way.

But when another citizen, trapped in a teen's body

for a thousand years, hugged me and cried into my shoulder, asking for my help to end this curse, I knew I couldn't be the smartest person here. But maybe, I would be the most human.

A few minutes later, both fulfilled and exhausted in equal measure, we followed Reign through the orphanage doors.

Volunteers greeted us, taking us along each separated section of the wide space and explaining their purpose. There were a few activity rooms and several children screaming as they ran from one spot to the next. While there was mischief, the absence of joy was palpable.

"We change volunteers every three months or so, rotating between those that are willing throughout the year to give them breaks. When we stayed with the same set of volunteers for extended periods, the toll was too much," the guide, Marie, explained.

"And you, Marie? How often do you take breaks from the orphanage?" Reign asked, hands behind his back.

"So kind of you to ask, Your Highness," Marie said. "I take off one week every quarter, to gather my bearings, then come back. Our volunteers are more than capable, but I want to help settle them in, so I don't switch off like the others do. I'm here for the adults and the children."

My throat tightened, and I had to blink rapidly to keep the tears back. "You are the bravest person here," I told her.

Marie nodded at me, lips tight. She knew it was true, but my recognition of it changed nothing for her. Only breaking the curse mattered.

Walking up the stairs, they showed us their dorms. Endless bunk beds greeted us, cramped so there was barely any walking space in between. We moved through the rows single file, seeing the stuffed animals and matching beds on each spot. My eyes trailed over each bed until I found one without a toy. When I saw a child sleeping, hugging a pillow, I placed the gifted bear beside them. In their sleep, they pulled the teddy to their chest with a sigh.

The walls were equally as cluttered, drawings on every available surface. There were layers of blowing papers, some done in crayon, others were finger painted.

Marie pointed out a few. "We clear the art every quarter as well, starting over. It's become a challenge for the kids, to see how quickly we can fill the walls."

"They are talented," Dre said, taking in the unique pieces.

We were about to leave for the next room, when

Queen Arika paused on the left corner of the room. There were several sketches beside each other, seemingly by the same child with their similar style. I couldn't see much from where I stood, but whatever the subject was must have left an impression on her.

She picked the sketches off the wall, taking the whole stack, and said to Marie, "I'd like to speak to this child. Can you direct me to them?"

"Of course, Your Majesty."

CHAPTER TWENTY-THREE

Queen Arika and Marie separated from the group to meet the child she requested, and another volunteer, Sheryl, continued our tour.

We entered the domed room at the top floor of the orphanage. Inside were two dozen wood cribs laid out in a U-shape. At the end was a set of rocking chairs by a window and a small shelf of children's books. An elderly woman sat, holding one baby in each arm as the chair moved.

Many of the babies were squirming in their cribs, soft cries filling the room, but there was something off about it. It was almost too quiet.

"The baby room is too difficult for most of our volunteers," Sheryl explained. "Very few people request to be placed here, but Lilian always comes back. Besides Marie, she is our most long-standing volunteer."

Lilian looked up and said hello, but we gestured for her to stay seated when she tried to get up and curtsy to Dre and Reign.

"Can I hold them?" I asked our tour guide.

"Of course," Sheryl said. "They could use all the cuddles you can give."

Taking the closest child in my arms, I cradled their neck and swayed. They leaned into my embrace, nuzzling closer.

"It's okay—" I looked at the nameplate on their crib, "—Sarah. I've got you, honey."

Eudora, Rosamund, and Amelia said hello to a few of the babies, running a hand over their brows and thanking Lilian, before following Sheryl out. I asked to stay behind, not willing to put Sarah back in her crib yet.

"Will you be alright here?" Reign asked as the rest of the group moved on. "Are you sure you want to stay?"

"Yes, I am, thank you," I replied. "Like Sheryl said, this is a hard room. If they are going to get less attention overall, I want to help here for the afternoon."

Reign smiled at me. "Alright." Wrapping an arm around my shoulder, he looked down at Lilian. "Thank you for all your work and care, Lilian."

Turning back to me, he kissed my cheek and put a strand of hair behind my ear. "I'll come find you when we are getting ready to go."

My cheeks flamed and I nodded, smiling back at him.

"Are you sure you and the prince aren't already engaged?" she asked with an amused grin.

"Not yet, Lilian. Ask again next week," I joked.

After some more teasing, we set on a quest. With my help, we aimed to hold each child, all two dozen of them, for at least five minutes each. We started on opposite sides of the room, meeting in the middle as we spent time with each baby, before starting from the beginning again. Hours passed and I felt all energy drain from me like a slowly souring milk. The babies felt what I felt, I was sure of it, my desperate yearning for their happiness.

But even with the way they cuddled into my arms, their unease didn't settle. It was not enough, no matter what I did. They continued to whine, coos of despair that were deeper than I thought they should feel for being so little.

"Is it always like this?" I whispered.

"Yes," Lilian said, brushing back the tufted hair of a baby. "Every day."

"How do you do this? Doesn't it break you?" I asked.

The baby in my arms grabbed a length of hair, tugging my face closer.

Her answer was immediate. "Someone should break for them."

It stopped me in my tracks. Someone *should* break for them.

Putting the last baby down in their crib after my second circle around the room, my gaze drifted to the window. The sky was gray, clouds filling my vision and the soft pitter patter of drizzle met my ears. It wasn't yet a downpour, but it would be.

"Babies aren't supposed to cry like this," Lilian commented after a while. "I'll be so happy to hear their crying change, once you break the curse."

"What do you mean?"

"In the times before, babies would wail for attention. You probably didn't see it, being so young before the curse. But babies should be louder. They know something is wrong with them, but they don't know what. These are the cries of children that don't know rest. They've given up."

Her words haunted me. I looked at the cribs again, truly stopped and stared. She was right. That was what was bothering me. They were unsettled, broken, with no way out. It was unnatural. *Babies should be louder.*

A hand dropped to my shoulder with a squeeze and I jumped, startled from my hazy thoughts.

"Your Highness," I stuttered. I hadn't heard the door open.

Dre smiled at me, white teeth bright in the low light. He was a statue of beauty. Despite my decision to pursue a partnership with his brother, I couldn't help the excitement I felt at seeing him again. Dre wanted nothing from me, not my hand in marriage or a crown to place on my head. When I was with him, I just *was*, and that felt rare.

"You've been in this room the whole day," he said, rubbing his hands up and down my arms. "You should take a break. We'll be leaving soon."

His presence made me shiver again. My body was always alert around him, like a flame trying to fight against an approaching storm. *It has been a long time...* I thought, then shook my head. *No.* I should stay here until we go. If no one else was going to help them, I should. They may not remember me, but I wanted these babies to feel that I tried.

"Thank you for your concern, Your Highness. The babies get so few visitors, so I'd like to stay until we leave."

His eyes narrowed. "You should take a break," he

repeated, more seriously the second time around. A little crinkle formed in the middle of his brow.

That's sweet, Dre must be really worried. We haven't seen each other in days, after all. I shook my head again but smiled at the prince as gooseflesh littered my arms. "Thank you for caring, Your Highness, but I promise I'm alright. I don't need a break."

Dre looked around the room, noting the slack-jawed Lilian watching our interaction. I quietly took a step back, his arms falling to his sides. We were a bit too close for people that shouldn't be that familiar with each other.

"Lilian, correct?" he asked with a tilt of his head.

"Yes, Your Highness," she said, wobbling into a curtsy.

He waved his hand, seeming to say it was unnecessary. "If you don't mind, dear Lilian, I would like to talk in private with our favorite Curse Breaker for a few minutes. Please leave us."

"Of course," she agreed quickly, walking out of the room faster than I thought she could given her slow movement around the nursery the past few hours.

Dre watched her, eyes narrowed, before coming back to stare at me.

We both waited a few beats after the door closed before turning back to each other.

"Why did you chase her away?" I asked. Poor Lilian has been working so hard, and doing this daily too.

"Because," he said, stepping closer and wrapping me in his arms. He dropped his head on top of mine, sighing. "I haven't seen you all week and I wanted to see if you were okay. I missed you."

Having his touch again was like transporting into another life. How could so much have changed so quickly?

"I'm okay, all things considered. How are you? I was so scared when you didn't come back."

"I'm sorry, Madeline. I was going out of my mind without you, but with all that happened I couldn't get away." He held me tighter, arms trailing down my sides until he gripped my waist.

"I missed you too," I whispered, pulse quickening. I gave myself a moment to feel him, but then said, "We need to talk, Dre."

He sighed into my neck, bending to kiss up my skin. "I don't want to talk."

"But we have to," I protested weakly, body tingling. "Things have changed—"

He interrupted my thoughts with a punishing kiss, tilting my chin up as he devoured my mouth. His other palm held my neck, not tightly, but in a possessive movement, caressing my collarbone, grazing the silver of my necklace.

My breath hitched.

"You like that, dear Madeline? You like when I hold you like this?" He held me tighter, over my pulse point as if he could count the beats of my galloping heart. "Don't think of lying. I know it's true."

Pulling back, I looked into his eyes and panted. Yes, I wanted more. I needed to feel his touch more than I've ever needed anything, but this wasn't a path I could go down any longer.

Dre looked like a wild man, unlike the flirting prince I was used to. He started to lean down again, seeking my lips, but I turned my cheek to the side, not giving in.

A mumbling cry sounded beside us and the spell broke, reminding me of the very inappropriate situation we were in. This was an orphanage, these children had no family but each other, and very little awareness of the hell their minds were repeating over and over.

I walked away from the prince and picked up the crying baby, soothing him with a gentle rocking.

"You're good at that," Dre commented softly, taking in my movements.

"It surprised me too," I said lightly. The baby squirmed and I tucked him in closer to my chest. "My neighbor has a toddler, Flora, but I don't know anyone with a baby this small. I admit, this has been one of the worst days of my life."

His voice was cool, despite how he stole my breath just moments before. "What makes you say that?"

"These babies are tortured, trapped in their small bodies, living the same day over and over again, without the capacity to change it. They may not be conscious of it, but their soul knows. Even if their brain can't keep up, the Ageless Blight has changed them. Who knows what will become of their development when they are able to age again..." It may be too late for them, but I had to try.

I hoped I was wrong, that they could recover from this, that we all could, but after these hours, I felt cynical in a way I hadn't been before.

I feared for these children, more than I feared anything else. Not even the Unending and what they may do scared me as much as the future for these kids.

After a few moments of silence, I looked up. Dre had turned from me, looking out the window like I had been. His face was pinched in concentration. As if he felt me watching, he looked back. There wasn't happiness there in his eyes. It was a steely focus.

Had he figured out what I was planning to say? "Dre—"

"I should let Lilian back in," he interrupted. "And we should join the others downstairs. It's time to go."

Something shifted in me as he walked away, but I couldn't pinpoint what.

I leaned over the cribs, saying goodbye to each baby before I left. One grabbed my necklace, and I pulled it from their tiny fingers. It must have fallen out with all the rocking.

Tucking it back under my dress, I thanked Lilian for her work, hugging her as tightly as she'd let me, and went to follow the royal family out of the orphanage.

We left with an additional number, a little girl, joining the queen's carriage. Her long blonde hair flowed down her small form, just shy of four feet.

In the little girl's arms, she held the drawings the queen had been interested in, a small backpack of belongings with that. Did the queen also love the arts, like Dre? Was she adopting her or just sheltering her?

One of the drawings fell, and Dre picked it up to hand back to her. Catching a glimpse of it, the picture showed two men atop a hill, fire surrounding them.

That night at dinner, the queen and the young girl did not attend. Asking Reign about her, he said she would become an apprentice to the prophet but wasn't being adopted by the queen.

Would the prophet adopt her?

I was fascinated by how that came to be, the queen noticing something in their drawings that reminded her of prophecies. What else did the girl say that showed they were true and not just artistic talent and an overactive imagination?

We'd all find out more soon anyway, meeting the prophet tomorrow and finally moving on to the second phase of this odd contest.

Dre avoided my eyes during dinner, leaving with Serena early into the meal. Somehow, I had to signal that I needed to see him.

I had given in to his kiss, a goodbye that was too deep and all encompassing between our moving bodies. But that's what it was, a goodbye. It was over, and I think he knew it, trying to keep me away as long as possible to prolong the inevitable.

How could something that was so brief in my life feel this painful?

Reaching for Reign's hand under the table, I held it tight. He glanced down at me, squeezing back with a smile.

"What did you just say?" I asked, adding myself back to the conversation. My future needed my attention, not the pull of the past.

CHAPTER TWENTY-FOUR

Walking into the dining room the next morning, after missing the morning wake up call, I yawned. I should still have a few minutes to eat, but it was so hard to get out of bed that I considered missing the meal entirely, despite my love for breakfast food.

"Good morning Madeline, did you sleep well?" Reign asked, pulling out a chair for me.

I looked at him blankly, my under eye bags on display. Sweeping my beige dress out of the way, I said, "Take a guess."

He chuckled. "I'll take that as a no."

Nodding, I said, "Sleep was difficult. I tossed and turned for hours. I couldn't stop thinking of the orphanage."

And of Dre.

Reign ran a thumb over my hand in soothing circles. "I know, me too. That's why it was important we visit, to remember what we are fighting for."

My eyes turned to Eudora. She didn't wear her lipstick today, the signature red replaced with her muted natural lip color.

"Good morning, Madeline," she said, no bite to her tone. Eudora picked up her water goblet, taking a delicate sip.

I narrowed my eyes in suspicion but didn't comment. Was she trying to prove she could be nice? Or was she as affected by yesterday as I was?

Rosamund and Amelia chatted away, no outward clue showing they minded that Eudora and I were beside the prince for the second day in a row. They continued on with their conversation, the prince chiming in occasionally, as we ate our meal.

Fifteen minutes later, Rowan walked through the doors, stopping in front of our group of five. The queen, Dre, and Serena did not show this morning.

"Ready, Your Highness?" Rowan asked.

Prince Reignold stood from his seat, gesturing for us to follow.

I grabbed a bacon slice and unashamedly bit into it as we left the table.

"The time has come, Curse Breakers," Rowan said as we walked toward the door of the dining hall. "You are to meet with the royal family's prophet, and then afterward have a private moment with the queen to more intimately discuss the future."

Looking down at the greasy food in my hand, I had immediate regrets. I thought we'd have until the afternoon, with plenty of time to emotionally and physically prepare. What if she needed to read my palm and it was covered in bacon grease? I turned and ran back to the table, dropping the last bit of the food and wiping my hands on a napkin.

Reign laughed and I glared at him for a second before schooling my expression. "Apologies," I said as I rejoined them at the door. Reign's hand went to rest on my lower back and I looked up to him questionably, but he didn't say a thing. The look on his face was endearing, a soft look just for me...

With everyone watching.

My face heated and I looked at Rowan, begging with my eyes for him to get us going. Rowan got the message and called everyone's attention, leading us out of the room while Reign stayed at my side.

"Have I told you lately how adorable you are?" he whispered in my ear, his voice soft with affection, as his hand rested on my back.

Shaking my head slightly, I looked up at him, my cheeks flushed with a shy blush. The giddy feeling filling my chest felt so unlike what I'd experienced before. It was a joyful happiness.

We stopped somewhere, but I wasn't paying attention enough to know where. I stepped away from the prince and took in the hall, walking to the other three Curse Breakers. Where were we? Amelia noticed my confusion and whispered, "Third floor."

Ah, that explains it, we were told never to come up here.

The stones appeared darker in this part of the castle. There were paintings and tapestries across the walls, with a space where a doorless room stood. Rowan explained we'd be going into that dark expanse, saying there was a long hallway and another door to enter at the end, with a second room within that one. The lightless hole felt unnatural in a way I couldn't explain.

It wasn't just a lack of light that made the hallway dark, but an expanse of magic instead, deep and encompassing.

Turning from it, I took in the art while Rowan confirmed if the queen and the prophet were ready for us. The tapestries had a more dangerous tone to them than in the other parts of the castle. One had stars above a burning forest. The fire had a blue center to it. One star had a wider twinkle to it, with a slight yellow hue. Another tapestry beside it was of a spinning wheel held in gold light.

My eye caught on a different tapestry where Eudora stood. I walked to join her and together we stared.

It was the castle at night. The windows were bleeding, trails of blood dripping until they created a red moat around the castle. In the sky, lightning struck between the clouds.

"Why would they commission this?" Eudora whispered.

"I don't know. Maybe it was a gift," I replied weakly. "Do you think all of the art in this room was made by the same person?"

We glanced at the collection throughout the room. While they had different subjects, the ominous feeling was the same.

"It must be," Eudora agreed.

Rowan clapped his hands and we turned our attention to him. "They will be ready for us in five minutes. Each of you will go in one at a time. In the first room, you'll speak with the queen, then in the second will be the prophet. I will let you know when it is your turn to enter," he explained. "As you all know, the line of succession comes from the queen's blood. Only the royal family and a few trusted advisors know the true identity of the prophet, so you are being given a gift by meeting them before your engagement."

Reign stepped in. "You cannot tell anyone the identity of the prophet if you leave here. And anything they tell you should remain a secret, only shared with myself, should you choose to."

A motion beside me drew my attention. Eudora was wringing her hands, more nervous than I'd seen her before. With each passing second, I felt more and more like we could understand each other.

We would meet the person who divined the prophecy that changed our lives. It felt like a final test, like everything we did up to now did not matter if this person did not approve of us.

I watched as Reign left to go to the other side of the rooms, waiting to meet Curse Breakers as they exited the other side. What would I know about myself and my future by the time I exited these rooms and saw him again?

"Come here, Eudora and Madeline," Amelia said, moving to stand in the middle of the room with Rosamund.

Glancing at each other, we did as she said.

"Let's take each other's hands," Amelia instructed.

Doing so, we formed a circle, four potential princesses together.

It was quite a moment as we stared at each other, different in so many ways, not just appearance. I drew a comparison to the Four deities.

Thailor, the steadiness of what time should be. That was Amelia.

Veyra, vindictive, taking souls regardless of whether their bodies were ready or not. While I knew the goddess was trying to take back the natural order of things, it felt angry, petty even. It felt like Rosamund and her judgement.

And then Eudora, who had a hidden kindness to her I was only now starting to see, hidden beneath her sensual nature, like Vexion, the deity of lust.

That left love, Miran. Was that me?

Or did I have it all wrong, and the goddess of love and beauty fell to Eudora, and I was Vexion, with my affair with Reign's brother?

Guilt coiled in me.

"I think we can all agree that after this, nothing will be the same," Amelia started. "Whether we know who wins the prince's hand or not after this, we'll know more about our place in this world after meeting the prophet."

Rosamund continued the line of thought. "No matter how annoying I find you all, I know this experience was something special, that only we will understand out of everyone in Riversend."

Eudora tightened her hand in mine. "Let the best woman win."

"No, not the best," I added. "Let the right woman for Reign win."

They murmured in agreement, standing in the circle a moment longer, before a bell twinkled in the distance.

"Curse Breaker Amelia, you are up first," Rowan said.

She broke from our chain, seeming more than happy to step into the dark hallway. It was eerie how her burnt orange dress was swallowed in the black.

Ten minutes later, the soft twinkling bell rang again, and Rowan instructed Rosamund to go next.

Eudora sat beside me on a small tufted couch, beneath the burning forest painting. She folded her hands over her knees. I glanced at her, but waited. After a minute, she spoke.

"Did you know about the—" she shakes her bracelet, "—before he told you?"

"It wasn't him that told me," I admitted, "but it was only a few days before you were told. I haven't known that long either."

Eudora folded her hands together, gripping hard, her knuckles leaching of color.

"Are you alright, Eudora?"

Her eyes flicked to mine and she swallowed. "I can't stop thinking about it. We've been told all our life about psychics, prophets, whispers of the secrets of witches, but this..."

I knew what she meant. None of the powerful people we knew to exist were able to control us, not like the mirrored Unending could. She was right, this was different.

"I know. Nearly half of our population are Unending, and if even a small portion of them could control us, it would be too many."

Glancing at me, she asked, "What if our destiny isn't just read, but forced?"

"What do you mean?"

"It's between us two, the Summer Maiden. Despite what Amelia and Rosamund think, it's not them. Of course, I'm betting on myself," she said confidently, "but it could be you. Is it *really* us? Or are we already puppets, forced to do things without our knowledge, and the jewelry is fake?"

I took her pale hands in mine, turning to face her on the couch. "We are protected now, as are Dre and Reign. They can't manipulate us. I can assure you the jewelry is real." Eliza would never lie about that, it was her blood protecting us whether Eudora knew it came from her or not.

"Dre?" Eudora asked, eyebrows raised, distracted by the familiarity for which I spoke of him.

"Prince Dredrick," I corrected quickly.

Her nervousness leached away, drawn in by her need to poke at me. "My, my, little Madeline, what friends you have."

"Shush, Eudora. Like you said, it's one of us." I agreed with her, sneaking a glance at the dark room that Amelia and Rosamund went into. "Let's stay on each other's side now, okay?"

"Deal," she said, pulling her hands away from mine, seeming more centered. "Now how do I look? Good enough to chat with a queen?" She pulled a small compact from her dress pocket, using the little mirror inside to apply the red lipstick she had been lacking this morning.

"As always," I said with a smile.

She finished her puckering and took in my appearance. "May I?" she asked, holding a powder puff to my face.

Eyes wide, I nodded.

Eudora blotted my face gently. "There, no more shine."

"Thank you," I said. "That was nice of you."

"If I had no competition, life would be boring. Give me a run for it, alright?" She stood, smoothing out her dress.

A moment later the bell rang, and she too disappeared into the dark.

When it was my turn, I looked at the darkened hall, standing alone. Dre's words came back to me from that first night in the palace.

"You will walk in there with your head held high."

The way he said it had instilled such confidence in me. While things are over, or would be once he stopped avoiding me, I was still grateful for that belief he had in me. Hoping to embody that strength again, I lifted my chin and stepped forward. Now was the time for answers, finally. I'd know who the prophet was and how I was supposed to end this.

The hallway stretched long and narrow, shrouded in shadows so deep that my eyes couldn't adjust. Each step was loud, an echo that signaled I wasn't alone in the hall.

Turning my head, I glanced behind me but couldn't see anything or anyone. It must be my imagination, my heart was beating so loudly it clouded my senses.

On my tenth step, a flame lit as if alerted by my proximity, illuminating a door as dark as the walls. I reached for the brass knob, before thinking better of it, and lifted my hand higher to knock first.

"Come in," a soft voice sounded through the wood.

Opening the door, my eyes struggled to adjust, blots of color clouding my vision until it settled in the low lit room. There was a fireplace, candles littered across many surfaces, and a circular table at its center. Despite the candles and the crackling fire, the room was cold. Impossibly, it smelled like rain.

"Sit, Curse Breaker Madeline," a familiar voice said. My eyes turned from the light to the seated figure. Incense released smoke plumes from the center of the table.

"Your Majesty," I said with a curtsy. I'd certainly gotten better at that in the last few weeks. I sat in the chair she nodded to, tucking in my ankles and adjusting my dress to sit comfortably.

The queen gazed at me, her blue eyes seeming darker in her sacred space, with her curls loose, creating a halo around her face. I blinked, getting lost in her stare, waiting for her to speak. Was she waiting for me to break first?

Before I could break the silence, she clapped and the room was engulfed in light. The candle flames grew higher, the fireplace roared, and a chandelier lit above our heads. Twinkling, the crystal cast celestial beams across the room.

I spun in my chair, watching the shrouded room come to life. With polished wood floors, stacks of books and papers, and sparkling crystals at each corner of the room, the essence of the room was completely changed. The crystals had the same quality as her necklace, a depth in their centers at odds with the rest of the glow, as if light didn't exist deep within them.

Turning back to the table of purple, red, and gold, I met the queen's small smile. Her blue necklace shined the most in the room, as if it stole the light she created, leeching it slowly. I glanced back at the crystal corners, then to the necklace again.

Narrowing my eyes, I felt like I should know something about these items. Her necklace had always stood out, its presence undeniable, but in this setting, with the other crystals to compare it to, I understood it was more impactful than a gaudy accessory.

The necklace held magic.

"Impressive, isn't it?" she asked, not about her necklace, but baiting for a reaction to her powers.

The question, and the presentation of her gifts, told me a lot about the queen. The woman we'd been told to stay away from...

She was insecure, grasping, and needed magic to feel strong.

"Very, Your Majesty," I agreed. While it was true, magic was always impressive, I also knew my agreement gave her what she wanted. "I didn't know you were so gifted in the art of magic."

"The line of the throne is very powerful," she said. "I've always known I'd be the one to wield that power."

"Why aren't your gifts shared with us more regularly? I'm sure the citizens would celebrate it," I asked. I couldn't wait to tell Hester about it, I'm curious what her opinion would be on it.

"Power is misunderstood," the queen explained. "Magic can do so much, yet not at all what you wish. A simple wish can become a nightmare, if you don't know the right way to ask for it."

What an odd way to phrase that, as if magic were a trickster. Remembering my first conversation with Reign, how there were drawbacks to being royal that I didn't know, made me wonder if this was one of them. Did Dre and Reign also have this power?

"I knew just enough, before the Ageless Blight, but in the years since I've studied my craft daily, honing it as it has honed me. But you are here to end all that, aren't you?" she continued.

"It would be an honor to help the Crown save the kingdom, but the Curse Breaking Committee has not told me how. Are you able to tell me, now that we are at the end of the competition?" Could I actually be useful now, please?

The queen scoffed, her breath pushing the plume of incense toward me. Sage and lavender filled my senses, making me sneeze.

Inelegantly, I waved my hands around my face, trying to clear the smoke. It burned my nose.

"Good," the queen said.

Blinking away my tears and sneezing again, I said, "I'm sorry, what?"

"The smoke detects the Unending. You would react rather differently to the smoke if you had already died," she explained.

Well, that was interesting. Eliza hadn't mentioned anything like that. Did she know about this trick?

"No, Your Majesty," I said patiently. "I am not an Unending. I wish to help them."

"Help them how?" she asked, that dark brow raising again.

"By ending the curse, letting them rest," I said, unsure of her meaning.

She pursed her lips. "That's not how some would answer."

I'm sure it wasn't. Especially now that I knew Eliza, and how people could hide in plain sight, it wasn't black or white. The dead had their chance, living a life beyond what their bodies should have, and now their souls were leaching from them, taking what makes them who they are. One day, if unchecked, no one would remain who they once were.

And the living would be in even more danger.

There were only two ways this could go—let the Unending take over entirely, eventually leading to the murder of everyone living, or end this curse and let the Unending pass, for good.

"How did you want me to answer?" I asked.

"It's a difficult question," the queen said. "On one hand, we are all frozen, unable to change. On the other, nearly half of our people are Unending. If they over-shadow the living, then maybe I should serve them instead. What do you think? If most of my people are no longer alive, then what must I do, as the woman that was raised to do what is best for the most people under her care?"

"I understand that perspective," I said slowly, trying

to buy time as I thought about what she would want me to say. This was a test, not a true conversation. Whether she admitted it to me or not, she wanted me to respond in a certain way. I couldn't speak as freely as I would with Reign. "I think that as the divinely chosen queen, the dominant ruler in your line, you should think through that, and whatever you lean toward will be the right answer. You'd know better than I would."

It was a cop-out answer, but I couldn't stop myself from adding, "But you also must consider the most vulnerable."

The queen reached for her necklace, stroking the gem. "Who do you perceive that to be?"

"The children at the orphanage and those that have been pregnant and waiting these thousand years. But it's not just about that. So many people, living and Unending, are suffering. Helping restore Thailor and the other deities would bring balance to the world again. We weren't meant to live this way."

Pausing, I tried to find the right words. In the ambiance of this ceremony room, the smoke between us, I felt like there was more beneath the surface than I could understand.

"Aren't you tired?" I asked. *I was.* As if the fatigue was bone deep, our stilted life drained me.

Queen Arika stilled, her eyes unfocused in the

distance behind me. After a moment, she said, "I grow more weary by the day."

"We're all in purgatory, Your Majesty. The Ageless Blight, this curse, should end." There, I've said my thoughts. She'd either agree or get rid of me somehow. There was nothing I could do if she didn't like me. "How do I end this?"

"You don't—" She gripped her necklace. "Only I can."

CHAPTER TWENTY-SIX

Between one blink and the next, the lights snuffed out.

"Your Majesty?" I asked, standing from my chair, hands braced on the table. "What is going on?"

I looked where she should be, edging around the table in the dark. When I reached her side, my hands met empty air. "Where are you? Can you light the candles?"

The room spun and I tumbled down, falling into the empty chair and then through it, as if slowly melting through its space in our reality. Hitting the ground, I felt damp grass where wood should be.

A galaxy of stars twinkled, spinning faster and faster until they streaked the sky. We were moving counter-clockwise so fast that my head couldn't keep up and I could barely keep from vomiting. I blindly reached around me for anything to hold on to. There was nothing.

Giving up, I laid down on the grass with my eyes closed, counting my breaths until I felt a change in the rhythm.

About one hundred breaths later, the world seemed to slow down, and I could open my eyes again. One star stood bright and solitary, a slight twinge of yellow to it, like in the tapestry of the burning forest. It did not spin with the rest.

Gathering my courage, I pushed up from the grass and walked in the direction of the star, keeping my focus on it as I tried to keep upright. I knew logically I couldn't reach it, but it was a steady point, and my only clue.

As if in response to my decision, the swirling stars slowed and eventually stopped, but my twinkling focal point remained. My legs grew weary, but I steadied on.

Lightning struck to the right of the star, a clap of thunder a few seconds later. There was energy in the strike that called to me, the sizzling it left in the air that felt cold yet welcome. It struck again, spidering waves of light across the sky. I looked at it, considering, then back at the star.

When the lightning appeared a third time, there was

a silhouette beneath it. I squinted, waiting for the light once more, making sure I wasn't imagining it.

It was impossible, but this whole situation was. When the light came again, I knew I wasn't making it up. It was the castle. I was in the middle of both tapestries, the star above the burning forest and the bleeding castle.

Would I also see the glowing spinning wheel?

I had a choice. While I didn't see fire yet, I knew if I followed the star I would find it. And the castle in darkness, lit by lightning, would bleed.

Which was better? Safer, even?

A fire was not controllable. At least, not by me in this magical hellscape. I could burn or suffocate.

Could I die here?

The crickets sounded real. The cold felt real. The hem of my dress had grass stains... Death seemed possible.

But the castle had blood on every surface, leaking through doors and windows. There was an uncertainty in not knowing what kind of death lay there. If I lived, the castle could be cleaned, but would it remove the stain? You'd always know it was there.

Just minutes before, I was in the castle, in a room of crystals with the queen. Should I go to the castle, blood and all, to get back into that room? Maybe I'd find my body there, and this was but my soul on an adventure. It could be part of the test, to find my way back.

Or was it?

A forest burning lays waste to what is in its path. It destroys habitats, lives, and if you survive, you have to start again somewhere new. Cleansing. Somehow I knew that was the right spot for me, to let go of all that once was for something new.

When the lightning sparked once more, I turned away. Back on the path of the star, I walked. Moments later, smoke began to crawl across the grass ahead.

Light shone behind me, trying to pull back my attention. The booms of thunder were louder than before, two seconds after each flash of lightning instead of three, as if it was angry at me for turning away, striking close until I agreed. I ignored it, leaving behind the cold for warmth.

Trees grew before me, sprouting up from the ground. They came up suddenly, with full branches already burning. Between each was tall grass, wildflowers, and one lone purple butterfly, flapping and confused.

Before it could get caught in the fire, I picked the flower the butterfly clinged to, bringing it close to me. I cupped my hand in front of it to shield the insect from the smoke. Above the canopy, the star shone brightly.

The butterfly came with me, small and vulnerable, as my limbs grew weary and lungs filled with smoke. It may have been my imagination, but I felt like I was getting closer to the star now. Could it be a mirage? Coughing, I followed, my vision blurring.

Between the burning trees was a hill. I moved toward it, picking up speed. The crackle of burning wood echoed, louder and louder as destruction took over. I picked up my pace, weaving through the trees, knowing if I wasn't fast enough I wouldn't make it out before they fell on me.

Fire licked my dress, spreading, but I dropped and patted it down with my free hand, cutting off its oxygen. My palm stung, but the fire stopped, and I made it through the last crop of trees.

Taking in pained breaths, I lay on the ground, staring up into the dark sky. The butterfly circled me, the flower having dropped into the fire at some point in the run for my life. Miraculously, the little being kept up, knowing to follow.

On the ground, I had a choice. Stay here, forget the star, and wait until it was all over. I'd already done enough in turning my back to the lightning, surviving the fire, and saving the butterfly. I could stop, right?

Minutes later, I didn't feel any stronger or calmer. But when the butterfly landed on my cheek and flapped its wings before flying away, it felt like a kiss. A thank you, even. I knew it was time to try again.

The fire had died, done with its dinner, leaving behind smoke, ash, and decaying trees. Not a speck of green between them.

The hill beyond it stood strong, lush, waiting for me to climb. Slowly, I made my way to the top.

The star seemed to float, descending from the heavens. I reached my hands up as if to catch it, like the butterfly. The air grew warmer as the star grew closer—it was not the same warmth as the fire, but a soft comfortable warmth that reminded me of peace. Its descent stopped when it was right between my hands, and I moved to encapsulate it, being sure not to move too quickly in case the star was skittish.

When my hands clamped around it and brought the star down to cradle it near my heart, it exploded into light.

I stumbled back in surprise, but just as I felt my body go into freefall down the hill, my vision cleared and the star disappeared.

Serena sat before me, back in the castle. The queen was nowhere to be seen.

"What was that?" I gasped, my voice scratchy and throat aching. I coughed, the burn of the smoke still prickling my lungs. But there was no butterfly, and no star. My head fell into my hands, exhaustion seeping deep into my bones.

It felt like hours had passed.

A little girl ran behind Serena, the one from the orphanage with matching blonde hair. She went around and around the table in circles, and my dizziness returned.

Was she the one spinning the stars? Or was it the world that spun beneath my feet?

Reign had said she would become an apprentice to the prophet.

Eyes flitting back to Serena, I asked, "Are you the prophet?"

She smiled softly. "I am."

Of course she was.

CHAPTER TWENTY-SEVEN

I t took me a minute to orient myself. The room was a near twin to the queen's chamber, but without the chandelier and crystals, and it was a little smaller. It may have been made for the use of the line of prophets that served the royal family, but I couldn't imagine anyone else shining in it the way she did. Serena was a beacon in the space, bright with her light hair, of course, but more so because of the confidence she held in every room she entered.

Was there anything about her that wasn't perfect?

"The queen..." I started, unsure what to say or how to describe the experience. "Are the Komari's prophets as well?"

"The queen is, but not the line as a whole," she explained. "The first and last in her line to have the sight, from what I can tell. And a witch, but that is a separate matter. Prophets are born, witches are made."

If she is so powerful, why need Serena at all? Was it Serena or Queen Arika that wrote the prophecy?

"Did she send me there?" I asked, focusing on my vision instead.

"Where did you go?" Serena asked instead.

Glancing at the grass stains on my dress, I said, "I was in a field, following a star."

"Did you succeed in catching it?"

I nodded, thinking of how warm I felt when it's light filled me.

She smiled, liking that answer. "I thought you might."

I tucked my hair behind my ear and took a deep breath, still reeling. The fire had felt like it would kill me. "What did it mean?"

"What do you think it means?" Serena replied.

Figures. "Do you always answer with a question?"

"Do you?"

"This is irritating," I muttered, standing to pace the room.

She smiled. "I find it entertaining."

The little girl laughed, continuing her run around the room.

"What's her name?" I asked.

"I'm Fauna," the girl answered before Serena could, her twinkling voice surrounding me.

It suited her to be named after a grouping of animals, and to be gifted with foresight.

How did prophets engage with Thailor? If you were able to predict what would come in the passage of time, did that threaten him?

Focusing on Serena, I got to the point. "I am not a prophet or a witch. I'm just a regular woman, wanting to move on with my life. Can you tell me plainly what I have to do next?"

"As the Summer Maiden, you turn the tides of time to your whim with your choices," Serena said. "It was unclear at first, but you accepted your path in this by choosing the star."

Her voice seemed so different from how I've known her so far. Selena seemed more free, playful, unveiled here as the prophet, than all the times I'd seen her as the future queen of the realm. Sure, there were some moments she had been friendly or flirty with Dre, but that didn't compare to now.

"I didn't though," I countered. "That was a vision. It wasn't real."

"Everything is real, Madeline. Every dream, thought, vision, nightmare. It's all happened. You chose the star. There was something else you could have chosen, right? And you ignored it?"

She didn't wait for my answer, just nodded as if she could feel my memory of the lightning storm I turned away from.

Okay, let's try being more direct. "How am I supposed to stop the blight, when the queen said only she could? How does that work in the prophecy?"

Serena busied her hands, picking up and shuffling the deck of tarot cards on the table. I hadn't noticed it, disoriented from the vision I was trapped in, but there was a rich velvet cloth on the table and a crystal orb that glowed faintly. A collection of tools used for divination —tarot cards, a small filled pouch, and a silver scrying bowl—surrounded it.

It was similar to the set ups I'd seen at fairs over the years, though I had never gone further than watching as other supposed prophets told fortunes to those that lined up. Serena's items all seemed higher quality somehow. There was a subtle glow around them, as if they held true power, or at least the residue of the power from Serena's hands.

I leaned forward, drawn to her movement.

"The queen is right that she is a defining character in the blight, but what she tries to ignore is how you will influence her." Her eyes lifted to mine.

"It's difficult for the queen to let go of her independence. She has been hurt and doesn't let people in easily."

"The king?" I asked, thinking of her late husband.

"In part, yes, but it's bigger than that now, as it was then," she said, continuing to shuffle.

"Why did Thailor abandon us?" I asked. "How could the queen and I get him to come back?"

Serena put down the deck, drawing three cards and placing them face down on the table.

She turned over the first, The Moon, with a dog and a wolf separated by a path leading to a body of water. They howled at the celestial body. At the end of the path was a castle split in two.

"Pain and choice are at the core of it, as is true for everything else. The queen was brought on this path because of an illusion of certainty," Serena said, tapping the tarot card.

She turned over the next. The Hanged Man. From a tree, a man hung by his foot. Despite the position, his face was calm.

"Surrender."

She turned the third, the Ten of Swords. A person lay prone on decaying grass, ten long swords stabbed into their back and legs. The sky was dark behind him.

"A collapse," Serena said, her voice solemn.

My eyes looked between all three cards. *The Moon. The Hanged Man. The Ten of Swords.*

While I wasn't trained in this practice, there was much to be said about intuition. "This isn't a very positive reading."

"No, it is not," Serena agreed.

"How do I stop this?"

"You aren't meant to."

My jaw clenched. "But that's why we are here, to break the curse." I quoted the scroll that started me on this path, *"For it's now or never to bring upon the prophecy."*

"That isn't the whole prophecy. We held some back, waiting for you to accept your path."

My heart plummeted to my stomach. I have been consumed by the words in the queen's scroll. My life may not have been a positive one, but it had been mine, until this prophecy came along. And now, I find out the words that claimed to determine my destiny were incomplete.

"*Who* are we?" I asked, the words laden.

"Myself, the queen, and Prince Reignold."

I noted that Prince Dredrick was not included. "And not the heir?"

Serena shook her head. "My fiancé does not know the full prophecy."

That seems like a lapse of trust to me, Serena, and your supposed fiancé. "Why not?"

"Because he has his own choices to make."

My eyes filled with tears. I closed them, letting a few fall as I tried to gather my thoughts.

Puppets. I was a puppet to play with. Myself, and Dre. People that thought they knew better than us controlled what we could or could not know.

I'd had enough. I was not someone they could manipulate whenever they felt like it.

They forced me here, played with my heart, and didn't even give me the whole truth of my supposed destiny.

I wouldn't stand for it anymore.

Serena reached for the pouch, but I stood before she could open it.

"No," I said. "I'm done here."

I walked past her, nearly tripping on Fauna playing with small white objects on the floor. When I reached the end of the dark hall and turned, I was temporarily blinded by the light. When my vision cleared, Reign and Eudora stood in front of me. He had an arm around her shoulders, comforting her as she shook. She seemed to be crying.

"He's a liar, Eudora," I spat as I walked, pointing at him.

"Madeline, wait, what happened?" the prince called. His arms still around her, Eudora looked up from his chest, her face splotchy.

Turning, I snarled at him. The prince I thought I could do good in the world with. "Don't talk to me again, Your *Highness*."

Clenching my jaw, I looked him up and down, taking in the image of the man that willingly blindsided me. The gorgeous man who had made me feel safe in his arms, encouraging me until I felt like maybe, just *maybe*, I'd be willing to be a princess.

The feeling was all gone now.

With a shake of my head, I turned and ran.

CHAPTER TWENTY-EIGHT

It's one thing when a prophecy tells me what I should be doing, it's another when a man does it.

I refuse to be bought, controlled, or caged.

Tears blinding my vision, I ran out of the wing and down the stairs. Ignoring Reign's calls, I passed the library, the kitchens, and made it back to the main floor. First, I'd go to my room to gather my things, then I would find Prince Dredrick. He'd know what to do.

I had to see him.

Breath ragged, I slowed down as I reached Curse Breaker Hall. Outside the wing entrance, I leaned against the wall, my forehead resting on the smooth wallpaper. Tears flowing, I gasped for air and the panic set in.

Nothing was as it seemed. Was our friendship ever

real? Did Reign just want to use me? I had to get my stuff and get out of here, preferably with Dre somehow. Maybe I could stay in his room while we figured out what to do next, or leave to stay in an inn.

My mind swam with possibilities, none of them great ones, and I began to feel faint.

"Madeline, what's wrong?" Dre said, stumbling upon me.

I looked up to the concerned eyes of Prince Dredrick. Victoria was beside him, hands politely folded in front of her.

"Your Highness," I whispered in greeting, wiping my eyes. "Hi, Victoria."

Mortified by my appearance, I covered my face with my hands, knowing there must be snot trailing down it. My chest heaved up and down, unable to meet an even rhythm.

Muffled, I asked, "Prince Dredrick, can I speak to you privately?"

His hands came up to take mine, pulling them down from my face. Without looking away from me, he said, "Victoria, can you excuse us?"

The blood rushing my ears lessened, and her foot-steps disappeared down the hall.

Dre took me in his arms, rubbing circles along my back.

I held him tightly, my tears staining his shirt.

"Tell me, sweet Maddy. What happened?" he whispered, pushing my hair back from my neck. He dropped a kiss on my clammy skin and I shivered.

"They lied to us, Dre. They all did," I whispered.

"Everyone is a liar at one point in their lives. We have lived a thousand years, after all. Who was it this time?" he joked, trying to lighten the situation.

"The prophecy—there is more to it, and they purposefully didn't tell us. Your brother, Serena, your mom." I choked on my words. "There is more and they didn't share it."

He froze, taking in this information. Pulling back, he lifted my chin.

"Who told you there is more?" Dre's words were slow, deliberate, as his eyes seemed to absorb mine. His thumb held my face in place, as if I'd ever look away.

"Serena," I said. "I know she is the prophet. She told me they held pieces back. Me and the other remaining Curse Breakers met with her, but I don't know if she told everyone or just me, because I'm—"

I shut my mouth tight, eyes widening.

He held my gaze. "Because you're what, Madeline?"

Swallowing, I allowed myself to admit it for a second time. "Because I'm the Summer Maiden."

Dre nodded, stepping back. Something unrecognizable flickered on his face. Not surprise, but something else.

"Right, my brother's impending bride. I knew it would be you." He scoffed and pulled away, facing the wall.

Without meaning to, I knew I'd hurt him. But this is what I came for, whether I was mad about it now or not did not matter. He knew, getting into this—whatever *this* was—with me, that I came here for his brother. Right?

"Did she tell you what was in the full prophecy?"

I shook my head, then spoke, realizing he couldn't see me. "No. I came straight to you."

In a swift motion, he turned back to me and grabbed my hips.

Gasping, I opened my mouth, and he cut me off with a breath-stealing kiss.

Chest to chest, I met his desperation, our mouths fitting together like he was my lifeline. My arms pushed down on his shoulders, jumping up. Legs wrapping around his middle, he moved to support me, gripping my ass with needy hands.

He turned us, and with a crash he had me against the wall of the very public hall. Why did it matter anymore, keeping this a secret?

With parts of the prophecy missing, the future was

mine. Summer Maiden or not, I was going to break this curse my way, with the prince of my choosing, and they couldn't stop me.

Gasping for breath, I reared my head back. Heaving, I gazed into his green eyes. They were bright, wild, wanting to devour me.

"Choose me, Madeline," Dre said, holding me up. "Throw the rest away. Imagine you walked out of that ballroom, away from the prophecy when I gave you the choice, and came back for me anyway."

Choices. Freedom. That prophecy made me feel like I had none, that it was all predetermined, simply because it painted Reign as this enthralled and newly wed figure.

But there was more to it. Maybe I didn't want to know what it was. If it would happen regardless, I'd rather feel like my choices were my own, that I would make them no matter what I knew or didn't know.

The god of age abandoned us. The world was suffering.

And I had a prince to kiss.

Nodding, I smiled at him, *choosing*.

With a laugh, he tugged my face back. Dre was wild, dangerous in the desperate joy he gave my lips. I moved with him, absorbing his energy. Either everything mattered or nothing did, and I was afraid to get to the root of that truth.

He pushed me into the wall, using it to keep me in place as he devoured me, hands running up and down from my ass to my thigh.

"I want you to be my goddess, Madeline. I'll do whatever you say if you let me stay between your legs. Will you grant me that?" Dre asked between kisses, trailing down my neck until he reached the spot at the top of my shoulder. He bit down softly, delicious pain hitting my system.

Quivering, I knew I'd give him nearly anything he asked for. He'd never lied to me or taken my choices away.

Dre kneaded my breasts, and as my breaths grew more ragged, I felt like I was falling down a waterfall while he held me tight, a lifeline. His length pressed against me and I gasped, wanting to give in, to let all our rules fall away.

"It'll be just us, Madeline, forever," he whispered in my ear, hand sliding up to my throat. He held it gently, nibbling my ear, but the effect was immediate.

Sobering, the adrenaline leaking from my body, I froze. Not from the hand, a deep part of me liked him holding me there, but that word.

Forever.

"We have to break the curse, together," I said, body shaking. Forever was over, it had to be. "I choose you, to help me break the prophecy. To take forever away."

His hand squeezed my neck, not too hard, like a reflex.

I dropped my legs, eyes narrowing, as his finger twined around my chain.

His eyes were dark. "Don't you think the kingdom deserves to live forever? To have unending opportunities?"

"We have already had that, for hundreds of years longer than we should have." I shook, all arousal leaving my body. "Thailor should return and grant us age back."

"It doesn't have to be that way."

"It does," I pleaded. "The children need us."

"There are more adults than children, shouldn't they be the deciding factor?" Dre said, pleading with me.

I pushed away from him, forcing his hands off me. In the middle of Curse Breaker Hall Wing A, the sconces were lit, casting soft glows on us.

Turning around, I looked at the door at the end of the hall, the last of the fifteen rooms in this wing. The door was left ajar, and I could see the painting above the bed.

Each room had a theme based on nature, Victoria had said. This one was a storm. Lightning.

In the vision, I had believed Reign to be the star in a burning forest. At the moment, I had believed it to be about renewal. Starting over.

If that was true, then the lightning above the bloody castle had been... Dre.

"Sweet Maddy, if I revealed the truth about us to the kingdom, would you be with me? As my queen?" he asked. "Forget about the rest of the prophecy, choose me."

Deep in my heart, I felt the crack. It widened, splitting me irrevocably in two. *For all and for each other, for one loves the other.*

I thought it meant friendship, that Reign would love me but that I wouldn't love him.

That wasn't what it meant. Or at least, not all of it.

Both princes may love me. I could love them, choose one of them even, yet I may stand alone. For all, for the people, without them.

Turning around, I faced the heir to the throne. The prince who was supposed to choose his kingdom. The man who had it all wrong, who would let children suffer, for his own misguidance.

Love was not like the books. This wasn't an Apes Matthews romance. The world should *not* burn for me, or for anyone, it should be saved for the vulnerable, to free them.

"No, I will not be your queen," I whispered, cutting off our future.

He snarled, walking toward me, a face twisted in an anger I had never seen before. "You dare say no to me?"

I recoiled, trying to widen the distance between us.

"Dre, we can't be together, not if you won't break the Ageless Blight. That isn't the future I want to have, I'm sorry," I said, trying to explain. "I care for you, but I can't do this."

"You were kissing me moments ago," he pointed out. "You chose me, you just said so, you can't take it back."

My eyes narrowed. How *dare* he? "That was before you admitted you liked things as they are."

He advanced forward, his height somehow larger than before. I felt the width of him blocking the hall, and my heart raced.

Faster than I could react, he grabbed my neck with one hand, the other curling over my chain. He lifted it, and my hands reached up to meet it, pushing back down.

"*Take it off,*" he yelled in my face, shaking me as he pulled.

Dread filled my veins. There is only one reason why he would want it off of me.

"What are you doing?" I whispered, fingers white as I pulled on his.

"Did Eliza give this to you? Who are you working with?" he demanded, tugging harder when I wouldn't let go.

The dead close in, Eliza had said.

I shook, struggling with him. He was going easy on me, wanting me to side with him, to give him what he wanted. If he used his full strength, he wouldn't need to struggle. Dre could break the chain or hit me and pull it off when I was distracted.

Instead, he let me fight him, trying to convince me.

Please, Dre, don't. Honor my choice. *No, don't let this be true.*

"You will not break the curse," he said, voice hard and vibrating, almost as if—

"Dre—" My voice cracked, my hands on top of his, not letting go. The goosebumps I was used to feeling around him rose again, my body running cold.

His eyes sought mine.

Green, gorgeous eyes.

The dead close in.

He let me go with a push and I slumped to the floor. My hands held to the chain, the necklace that protected me from the influence of the Unending.

The dead close in.

It echoed. The pain, the horror, what felt like could be the end of everything I knew. My heart, my soul, did anything actually matter?

"Let's not beat around the bush," Dre said, pacing in front of me. He reached under his shirt and pulled out a necklace of his own. In our secret meetings, we never went further than kissing and over the clothes touching. He may have touched my neck, but I never touched his.

Under his shirt had been a long chain like mine, but instead of a vessel for blood, it had a blue stone. It matched the queen's, but smaller.

His pacing increased, like he was a caged tiger with nowhere to go.

In a state of agitation, he shook his hands out, the necklace bouncing on his chest. He muttered, but I couldn't hear what he said.

"Tell me," I asked, tears running freely down my face. I knew what he would say, but I had to hear it, had to know without a shadow of a doubt.

"I want you to choose me, Madeline, not my brother."

"And?" I pressed, holding my breath.

He turned, pulling his hair, messing up his usually perfect appearance. Crouching in front of me, he pulled the necklace with the stone off. It fell to the floor with a clank, his eyes closed.

Dre shivered and he itched his collar, stretching it.

My eyes followed the movements, gasping as black veins climbed up his neck. Slowly, they descended until it was undeniable what I was seeing.

"Poison." His necklace cloaked it, magic keeping him undetected.

Magic the queen must have wielded.

"Poison," he agreed and opened his eyes.

Yellow eyes.

"If you lift the Ageless Blight, I die. For good."

The dead close in.

Veyra had his soul. Eyes once blue like his mother's merged with yellow to the deception of green.

"Die for me, Madeline. And *live*, forever."

CHAPTER TWENTY-NINE

The heir to the crown was Unending. A mirror, even, with his yellow eyes, able to control the actions of others.

Had he ever used it on me?

"Die for me," he repeated. "Stay with me, forever."

I wanted to deny it. Hoped, in those frozen seconds before it was undeniable, that there was another reason why he would want my necklace.

But Eliza had warned me. The dead recognized each other. She had known, from the first dinner in the palace, that the heir was gone. He had recognized her too, and who knows who else.

Dre inched closer and I fell back, my heel skidding against the stone. There was no space to mourn, not yet, there was only fear. He gripped my shoulders tightly, leaving nowhere for me to turn.

I wished for my dagger with a desperation that made my stomach heave. After everything Eliza had said, why hadn't I kept it with me? My training flashed through me—the hours of bruised knuckles and repetition until my muscles knew how to defend me without thought. All of it was useless now because I had been careless. I had trusted him, and ended up cornered against a wall for it.

"You don't have to do this," I whispered, my words drowned by the thunder of my own heart.

Veyra had his soul. He couldn't be trusted, but I still wanted to, more than anything.

His face blurred against my vision, his breath hot on my cheek. "You spoke of the vulnerable, Madeline. What do you think I am? Don't you want to be with me? Save me?" Dre's voice was desperate, pleading, hoping to be picked.

"Dre, the prophecy—"

"*Don't*—" he snarled, shaking me until my head cracked against the wall. Pain bloomed white-hot, making me gasp. "—talk to me about prophecies, when they have built my demise."

Minutes before, I had wanted the choice, angered that I didn't know what the prophecy said. But no matter what, my hopes were clear. End the curse. No matter what any prophets said, with a prince or without one, that was my aim. I wanted those in the orphanage to have their time, to decide their dreams, to find love.

Saving them meant killing Dre. Killing Eliza. Thousands of others. Somehow ending this curse with the queen and her mysterious powers.

And I would still do it, even if it meant destroying what was left of me. If I never had my chances, my autonomy, that would be okay, if my sweet neighbor could solve the puzzle box and truly live.

Take it all away. Miran, goddess of love, please blind me. Shelter me.

The prince paused, staring at my welling eyes.

"Madeline," Dre whispered, his voice softening, using my tears against me. "This doesn't have to be the end."

How could it not be, when my heart was breaking?

"Be with me, forever. You and me, we can rule together in the Deadlands. Two crowns. We can leave my brother to the living, until there is no one left but the Unending." His thumb ran along my lips. "Die with me. *Stay* with me."

When he dipped down, taking my mouth with his, I let him. Tears streaking, the salt trailing into our kiss, we lingered there for a moment. Yesterday, I had given him what I thought was our goodbye kiss.

That goodbye meant so much more now.

His fingers went into my hair, tugging me closer, and I yelped at the sting from my hit against the wall. His grip shifted, strong fingers clamping around my throat tighter than during our intimate moments. I gasped, clawing at him. "Let go—"

He kissed my eyelids, my forehead. "Rule with me."

"No, Dre, please." I gasped, the column of my throat compressing, barely able to get the words out. "Let's talk to your brother together, please, we'll work together."

"*Reign,*" he whispered, gripping me tighter, taking my breath. "You told me just minutes ago that he betrayed you, kept secrets from you, and you choose *him?* You speak of what is best for the kingdom, but the numbers aren't behind it. We can give the children forever death, end their suffering, and leave only those who want to stay."

My blood ran cold and my hands fell, limbs tingling. He continued to talk, unaware or uncaring, or even *enjoying* my destruction.

The children, the babies I held for hours, the team of volunteers that cared for them. He wanted to kill anyone that got in his way.

Dre wasn't the prince I thought he was. Maybe

before Veyra got to him it would have been different, but not now. Not when he berated me for not choosing him over the world.

Not when we could have been the world to each other, until our last moments, saving society in our last breaths.

With a start, possibly in the delirium of my lack of oxygen, I realized I would have died for him if the situation had been different. If he helped me with the curse, saved the kingdom with me, knowing it would take him from this plane of existence... I might have followed after the task was done.

But anyone who tried to take my choices from me did not get to keep me.

Weakly, I repositioned my legs on the floor, pulling my knees into the space between us. My vision grew spotty, panic flaring, but I had to focus.

With the last bit of strength I had left, I pushed my arms into the crook of his elbow to get leverage over his grip. "Stay away from me," I rasped and kneed him in the balls.

He dropped his hands, eyes wide, and I ran past him, holding tight to my necklace.

I slammed into my room, fumbling the drawer beside my bed open. The dagger Jake gave me was there, cold and blessedly sharp. I held it in my right hand, and

I shoved the small royal family book into my pocket. He didn't want me to read it, saying he'd be my royal tutor those weeks ago, and I needed to know why.

I stared at the lone pocket for a beat before slamming the drawer shut.

Racing, I left the room and ran back out of the hall, knowing my life depended on my speed. He wanted to control me, manipulate me, make me his. I wouldn't let him.

"Come back here, Madeline," Dre called, feet pounding behind me, catching up quickly.

A door opened, and Victoria reentered the hall from one of the Curse Breaker rooms. Catching sight of me and Dre, she seemed calm, unsurprised by the events.

Endless Ally.

"Stay," Victoria said, hands out. "It's okay."

"Get away from her," Reign's voice thundered in the hall. "Madeline, get behind me."

Turning, he was there, ready to fight, in the same stances I'd seen him in during training. For me.

I tumbled, reaching for him, my knees scraping the floor through my thin dress. He helped me up and I whimpered, clutching to his shirt.

"Your brother," I choked out, throat burning. I aimed the blade out toward the hall, drained but knowing this was far from over.

Reign's gaze snapped to Dre, who stalked closer, yellow eyes burning.

"Brother," Dre snarled, voice warped with hatred. *"Give her back to me."*

"Would you run if I told you to, baby?" Reign asked, hand on my wrist, eyes flitting back and forth between his brother and me, too calm. His voice was steady, but I felt the tremor in his fingers, centuries of sibling rivalry and royal politics pressing against his choice. His calm wasn't calm at all.

I wouldn't leave him.

With a confidence I didn't feel, I said, "Not unless you come with me."

"Thought you'd say that." Reign dropped down and grabbed my legs, hoisting me up.

I yelped, holding on as he threw me over his shoulder. "What are you doing?" I angled my weapon away, protecting his back.

"Saving you," he said, holding me tightly and sprinting down the hall.

The words sank into me, tattooing my heart. Saving me, not the kingdom, not himself, *me.*

Moving faster than I thought possible, he sped us out of Curse Breaker Hall. Bouncing on his back, I watched Victoria and Dre run after us, faces twisting.

She ripped something off her hand, putting it into a pocket.

Her hazel eyes morphed, now matching Dre's. They shrieked in unison, as if they were one mind, running after us, their arms pumping at their sides. They gained ground quicker than I thought possible.

They were predators, and Reign and I were prey.

"Let me go, I'll slow you down," I said, gripping his shoulder. If he died because of me I'd never forgive myself.

Reign ignored the request, breath ragged as he tore down the corridor and out the plaza doors. Rowan looked up, a clipboard in hand. Mitchell and Eudora were with him. Wide-eyed, they asked what was going on before Dre and Victoria barged in.

Mitchell jumped up without hesitation. "Run!" he screamed at Eudora and put himself in front of Dre's path. Pulling his arm back, Mitchell punched the prince with a crack that reverberated on the stone floor.

"I've always wanted to do that," he said with a laugh, adding in a kick.

Eudora said something I couldn't hear, drowned by the sound of flesh hitting flesh and Victoria's scream as she jumped on top of Mitchell.

Dre wouldn't stay down long, I knew that, and Mitchell's distraction could be his last moments. I struggled, trying to get down and help, but Reign held tighter as he raced past the chairs and out of the plaza. He didn't stop at the garden of de-thorned roses, instead running to the gate beyond it. Guards were positioned along it, keeping the perimeter of the palace safe.

"The heir needs you, attend to the future king!" he screamed, pointing the direction we came. Without missing a beat, they pulled out swords and ran.

Reign let me down, gripping my hand, and I trailed along until we reached an opening, similar to the entrance into the palace grounds. The security room attached to it was empty, the guards likely alerted by our screams moments before.

We ran past it, off the path that held supply wagons full of food, gardening equipment, and other items that must come through the back so as not to distract from the beauty of the castle.

Branches clawed at us, leaving scrapes on my arms as we jogged. He slowed down when I tripped on a root for the third time but didn't let go of my hand.

"What are we going to do?" I asked.

We walked for a few minutes before he answered, the sweat running down his brow. His eyes were on alert, shifting across our path and behind us.

"I have a place in the woods, we're almost there," he said and finally stopped. He pulled me behind a large tree, encouraging me to lean against it to catch my breath. "Less than a mile to go."

Running a hand through his sweaty hair, he said, "Dre and my mother don't know about it, and it's protected magically from their detection, for the most part—my mother is a bit of a wild card. But I prepared it years ago, in case something like this happened."

Closing his eyes for a minute, seeming to center himself, he opened them and took me in. My grass stained dress, the scrapes on my arms, messy hair, and then stopped, focusing on my neck. My hand went up, touching where I knew I must be starting to bruise.

"Baby," Reign said, coming closer. He gently grazed the skin, his lip quivering. "Did—" He paused, swallowing. "Did he kill you?"

His eyes welled with tears. Crying, for me.

"Reign, no. I'm alive, I promise."

Pulling me into a hug, he held me tighter than he ever had before, his head dropping to my shoulder. Taking in deep breaths, Reign tried to control his emotions, but the tears fell.

"I'm so sorry, baby. I'm so sorry," Reign murmured, holding me like I was precious to him.

I held him back, because I knew in my heart I felt the same.

"Reign, he said horrible things," I said, still locked in

our embrace, throat pained. "How he would let you rule over the living for now, until there was no one left but him and the dead. He said—" I paused, almost unable to voice the cruelty of it. "He said he would kill the babies, children, and anyone else too vulnerable to continue. Permanently."

"He won't succeed Madeline. He can't have you, the kids, or the kingdom." His hand stroked my cheek. "I promise."

Voice cracking, I whispered, "I don't think you can promise that."

"You're right. I can't guarantee anything. But I've got you, Madeline. I told you, didn't I?" His smile was small, but there. "Not even destiny can keep us apart."

I shook my head, that moment at the ball feeling so far away. "But you lied, Reign, about the prophecy, and who knows what else. I want to trust you, but how can I?"

He nodded, knowing I was right after everything that's happened. "I'll earn your trust back, Madeline. Starting with the prophecy."

Stepping back, he extended his hand. "Let me show you my home, and I'll tell you everything."

I looked at him, standing before me, asking for another chance in the expanse of trees before us. Miles behind us, a castle turned to blood. I knew what to do, but I had one question before I could take it further.

"What about Mitchell and Eudora? What happens to those we left behind?" Their faces flashed in my mind. Eudora crying before I ran to Dre. Mitchell's glee as he willingly put himself between us and danger. Are they okay? What were the queen and Serena doing with this turn of events?

The prince smiled at me, his eyes soft, like he was proud I cared to ask. How could I not though?

"Mitchell knows what to do. He has been in on my plan the whole time. Knowing him, if Eudora is safe, he'll bring her into it. And if he doesn't, we'll ask him once he meets us back here."

I sighed, taking his hand. "That's good to hear. I'm glad he is someone you trusted too."

His grip on my hand tightened. "I have a lot to tell you, Madeline. I'll admit I have a lot of secrets. Mitchell is one of them."

"What do you mean?" I asked. We began walking, the sun descending around us, its colors spilling across the sky, casting halos among the trees.

With a laugh, he said, "He's my half-brother. And Apes Matthews."

Blinking rapidly, my mouth parted, dumbfounded.

"I know. I'll tell you everything, I promise. But first, let's get inside." He tugged my hand and I walked beside him. The trees began to clear, becoming less dense than before.

"Inside whe—" I started, before I spotted it.

The silhouette of a quaint cabin, about the size of my own in Everbrook, was visible through the trees. A trail of pebbles led up to the house, a pathway to keep the grass and weeds from taking over the entrance.

"Welcome to my hideaway," Reign said sheepishly.

My body slumped, Reign catching me with an arm around my waist. I leaned my head on his shoulder, taking the strength he gave me.

"Madeline, are you okay?" he asked before swearing. "No, of course you're not. I'm sorry, that was a dumb question."

Shaking, I couldn't speak. We survived, getting away from the castle and all that was within it. My brain was overwrought, unable to process anything other than the fact that we could stop running. Delayed in the forest, not yet in the clear, the reaction hit me now that there was an end in sight.

We're okay. We made it. Reign is okay. Somewhere safe. With him. Together.

My thoughts barely formed, fragments flashing across my consciousness.

"I've got you, baby," he whispered, taking me into his embrace for my turn to break down.

I held him back just as tightly, allowing myself to feel more than the need to survive. The fear was still there, the unknown hanging over me, but the immediate danger was gone. Paused. For now.

The tears came fast, wracking my body until I could barely hold myself up. Reign held me through it, keeping me up against him. Whispering soothing words, running a hand down my hair and back, he comforted me until the shock faded.

"I'm sorry," I said after a time, each word becoming more painful now that I had the space to truly feel. "I don't know what came over me."

"Don't ever apologize to me, Madeline. I am the one that should be apologizing to you. Let's go inside, okay? Rest, then we'll talk."

With a nod, I let him lead me into the safety of his home, his arm braced around my shoulder like he couldn't let go.

Together, we'd face whatever came next.

Continue reading for an epilogue in Reign's POV.

EPILOGUE

REIGN

The woman of my dreams was asleep before me. Hair strewn about, wearing my clothes—an old shirt and large soft pants tied at the waist. Her small feet kicked off the end of the blanket so she wouldn't be too warm. The fabric swallowed her, the faint rise and fall of her chest barely visible in the low light. Outside, the wind rattled the windows, the smell of pine making its way through the gaps in the wood.

My small cabin hideaway had two bedrooms, but we shared one—not for any provocative reason—for safety. She said she needed me close or she wouldn't be able to sleep. I felt the same.

Even now, with her an arm's length away, the fear of losing her gripped me. What could have happened left ice in my veins. I had so much to tell Madeline. Things

I've never told anyone. The duality of it was a funny thing. I dreaded the conversation, and in equal parts it thrilled me.

She chose me, but it was under duress. In the back of my mind, I couldn't help but wonder. If my brother hadn't snapped, would she still have picked me? Or would she have become the queen of the Unending?

The Ageless Blight clung to us. Old souls in ageless bodies. Anyone with a completely stable mind in this was a miracle. Sometimes I wasn't sure it was possible at all, and that Veyra stole our souls in pieces, until everyone eventually fell to insanity.

We couldn't survive like this much longer.

My Madeline, my baby, no—just *Madeline*, I corrected myself. She belonged to no one, least of all me. She was attacked by the man she ran to after *I* hurt her. Madeline chose Dre first, my brother, the man I knew was Unending and didn't warn her about.

She had no reason to forgive me for that.

Looking down at her sleeping form, I brushed a strand of chestnut hair away from her face. At least she felt safe with me, even after everything she went through because of my family, she still trusted me.

And seeing her in my clothes? Asleep in my bed? The feeling in my chest grew larger, warmth spreading. Even without giving it a name, I knew what it was.

I've been alone for so long. Alone with the knowledge of my brother's death and all that it would mean. For me and the kingdom.

Would she have stayed if I had told her the moment I suspected things had started between them?

The prophecy. That *damn* prophecy. It said she had to choose, and I wanted her to have that choice. I didn't want her to feel forced into being with me.

But maybe she did anyway. Madeline was too kind to say no to what was best for everyone. She said she wouldn't be a good princess, not wanting the spotlight—but she was more suited for it than a selfish man like me.

Her bruised throat was more visible now, hours later. My fingertip grazed it, committing to memory the horror my family brought onto her. Dre, mom, Serena even... Now that Madeline made her choice, my mom needed to work with us to end this. Would she help me, or Dre?

I didn't know what to do next, or who to trust other than Mitchell.

Assuming he was still alive.

Madeline's eyes fluttered, awoken by my touch. She gazed hazily at me. "Is everything okay?" she whispered.

"Yes, everything is alright," I said. "Go back to bed, baby."

"Only if you do." She drew back the covers, inviting me into her warmth.

Slipping under the comforter, I pulled her back to my chest. "I'll protect you, Madeline. I'm so sorry."

She sighed, already drifting back into her dreams, settling against me. For the first time in years, I let myself relax. Not because I believed we were safe, but because holding her made me brave enough to pretend.

***

Thank you for reading *The Courting of Kingdoms*. Please take a moment to leave your thoughts on your favorite review platform and your purchasing retailer. Your review helps other readers like you find the series.

Not ready to leave the Komari princes behind? Read a bonus chapter from Dre's POV exclusively on rksampson.com/newsletter

ACKNOWLEDGMENTS

I never know what to write in the acknowledgments. And sometimes I skip them! On the surface, thank you messages typically go here. I work with very few people, and keep a small social circle, so that would make this list fairly short. However, there is a little more I want to add today.

To my husband, Chris, who has always supported me and believed in my craft. Thank you for being there for me and helping me prioritize my writing each weekend. I'm so grateful we get to live this life together, in love for more than half our lives. To my editor, Kïrsten of Unbound Literary Editing, for caring about my stories, rather than doing the job and moving on. My son, Jack, who thinks writing books is a normal thing moms can do, since it's all he's known me to do. I love that creativity is normal in my little family. To my friend and fellow author Sarra Cannon—our daily chats mean the world to me, because no idea shared between us is ever too big to go for. That's a rare quality.

But truly, in this note, I want to talk about the drain. The year and a half it took me to write this book was one of the hardest times I've had in a while. I'm no stranger to hard times, and unfortunately have had more than a few medical emergencies in the past decade, but these recent years weren't just a worry of physical danger, but an emotional fear that seeped into my creativity. This persistent worry for myself and my family ate away so much happiness this year, and breaking from that fear has taken active effort. It's not totally gone, but as I finally get this book into the world, I'm coping more, and finding that love again.

When you are in fight, flight, or fawn, it's difficult to think. Some people get more creative through fear, having it drive them to move forward, but when it's coming at me from all areas of my life, my ability to make decisions suffers.

Writing for me is an act of decision making mixed with an exploration of feelings, while crafting a world that doesn't exist. With ADHD and anxiety, using my brain for creativity was a struggle I couldn't manage for months.

But persistence is my biggest strength. I encourage you to hone it too. Persistence isn't the same as drive. Drive can be motivation based, while persistence is like a petty grit. Holding on tightly, as tornadoes roll through, stubborn enough to think you are stronger than the winds of change.

No dream is a failure if you have persistence at your side. Being an author is an act of choosing, again and again, to keep going. The longer you do it, the closer you get.

Some authors win out of the gate, and in a way that can be harder, because the pressure starts from the first book and builds.

The slow rise I've felt over these years built my muscles. I'm still there, over ten books in, prepared to keep going.

Are you willing to persist through the storm? Acknowledge that for yourself today. Only you can choose it, because it has to be chosen again and again.

I hope you enjoyed *The Courting of Kingdoms*, the book written bit by bit, as I moved through fear. Mind if I remind you again to leave a review?

Rebecca

ALSO BY R. K. SAMPSON

For the most updated list of titles

by R. K. Sampson, please visit

rksampson.com

ABOUT THE AUTHOR

R. K. Sampson is a YA and NA fantasy author. Her favorite scenes to write are plot twists, betrayals, and unique takes on love in fantasy settings.

She writes novels that help readers take on scenarios that can seem insurmountable like swift change, massive responsibility, and being different through the backdrop of magic, creatures, and flawed characters.

Rebecca is a mom and married to her high school sweetheart, living in Miami, Fl. You can read her blog chronicling her life and interests on rebeccaksampson.com and read her author life behind the scenes on rksampson.com. She writes nonfiction under the name Rebecca K. Sampson and paranormal romance as Rachel H. Drake.

instagram.com/authorrksampson

tiktok.com/@authorrksampson